# FOREVER CLAIMED

## A PARANORMAL SHIFTER ROMANCE BOOK ONE
## FOREVER LOVED

## L. J. HAWKE

*To my editors, critique partners, alpha and beta readers, amazing cover artist, and most especially my fans, thank you. You make my world rock.*

# PARTY ON

## EPILOGUE

Corinne Jackson was absolutely not happy about having to go to Sigma Sigma. Sigma Chi was boring, everyone in togas, dancing and pouring beer down each other's throats. It was so '80s movie, and Corinne couldn't drag her friends Kandace Walker and Tania Brussell out of there fast enough. They had agreed to say goodbye to absolutely anyone who had been kind, listened to them, pointed something out, pushed any of them in the right direction.

Steve with the hair was there, looking like a Roman senator in his toga, gesturing with the beer in his hand. Steve with the hair was actually less interesting than Steve with the buzz cut. The buzz cut one was planning on entering the military and was set to leave the next morning for Camp Lejeune. Steve with the hair got some sort of lawyer job at a firm in St. Louis and was drunkenly telling everyone about his planned trip to Europe. But, hair-Steve had helped Corinne during their Habitat for Humanity phase, so Corinne thanked him and handed him another beer. She walked toward her soul sisters and said, "We're out of here, my friends."

"Damn," said Kandace. "I was waiting for them to play 'Shout' and have us all lay down on the floor."

"Did you get a good look at that floor?" said Tania. "Not something

I want to be laying on anytime soon. Come on. Sigma Chi has real drinks."

And, they did. They had a tropical theme going on, helpful during a sticky Missouri summer. Corinne and Tania poured their tequila-infused electric blue lemonades over shaved ice, and Kandace pulled out a bright blue drink from her refrigerated backpack in order to fit in. They did some dancing to a steel drum band. "Where in this holler did they get the band?" Corinne asked the ladies.

"Kansas City Jamaicans," said Tania, twirling the umbrella in her drink. "Name of the band," said Tania, "Not where they're from." Kandace snorted. Sean decided to drink with Tania, and they swayed in a corner.

"That privy-face has had the hots for Tania this whole time," observed Kandace. "He's short, greedy, and sweaty. And that's on a good day."

"Harsh," said Corinne. "He's also nice to animals and small children."

Kandace laughed. "I'm sure he reads to children and volunteers at the animal shelter." She narrowed her eyes at Corinne. "I'll also make a bet you didn't see him at either place."

Corinne shrugged. Coding took an enormous amount of her time. So did Web design, creating databases, sharing a copywriting class with Tania, and taking photography with Kandace and Tania, the only class all three of them had together.

The last semester had been seriously crazy. Corinne had gone for her computer science degree because that's what her parents wanted, and she might as well get some damn money out of them after everything she'd been through. She still had college loans she had taken out to help her friends. She also pieced together some scholarships and had been steadily working with web design clients for years. Her parents had no idea of the type of life that she had, and they actually didn't care. They traveled, especially during the holidays, so Corinne and her friends doubled down on college classes and took on jobs over the summers, trying to get out of college faster. They worked their way all the way through to graduate school in five years.

Corinne was also part of a program to get old, comfortable chairs for dog shelters, so people could imagine cuddling up with a dog on a cold winter night. Corinne also brought dogs to school to have children read books to the dog. Dogs listen to whatever you say, so children with trouble reading, speaking, or extreme shyness came out of their shells with the reading to the pups. A lot of the rounds they were making on their last night together since they graduated that morning were to thank animal-shelter volunteers like Penny, who was dancing with Annabel and Georgia, and Jasmine, who had her tongue down Paulie's throat.

Corinne sighed, sucked hard on her drink, and went to go dance with Penny and thank her. Penny, a shy goth with dyed raven hair and a crimson smile, gave Corinne a hug, spilling half of her drink. Corinne was able to jump back in time to avoid the flow of liquid onto her feet. "Oh my God, this is so great, and I've got a job at the Comic Rube!" The Comic Rube was a publishing group for comic books, and Penny was a talented artist.

"Awesome!" fake-screamed Corinne. "Annabel, did you get the internship at the gaming place?" Corinne didn't name the gaming company because Annabel had applied to at least twelve of them.

Annabelle, another goth, raised her right pinky. "San Fran," she said, in a bored voice. Annabelle was perpetually bored.

Corinne tossed her head, the closest she could get to boredom. "Georgia?" Corinne said, hoping to not have to engage Georgia in conversation. Georgia had the brains of a flea, but was absolutely gorgeous, with cartoonishly large baby-blue eyes and raven-black hair. And the gazongas to go with, of course. She looked like an anime character, and knew it.

"What?" asked Georgia.

Annabelle rolled her eyes. "She didn't catch your question. Georgie here has a job working for her father's company in advertising," Annabelle said, her voice dripping with sarcasm. The other two girls were dressed in black bustiers and black-and-red-checked short skirts, and Georgia was dressed in a pale pink summer dress, making her look like a peach hanging on a black tree.

"That's nice," said Corinne. "I've got to go; my girls want me. Thanks again for volunteering, Penny," she said, and managed to avoid getting the rest of Penny's drink spilled on her when the girl attacked her with another hug. Corinne extricated herself to go say hello to Jasmine.

Jasmine, who called herself the token black woman behind everyone's back, had long, dark, lustrous hair, the kind that Penny and Annabelle would kill for. She wore red shorts and a blue jean top with no sleeves, and looked like a million dollars. Paulie, her girlfriend, was tall and thin, with short black hair and black eyes. Paulie wore a jean skirt and a red top, and the two of them had their arms around each other's waists. "Thanks for volunteering, Jasmine," said Corinne. "I hear you adopted one of the dogs from the shelter."

"Got married last week," said Paulie. "Thought my wife would like someone to play with when I'm out building houses." Paulie vastly underestimated herself. She was actually a very gifted architect.

"How's the urban planning thing going?" Corinne asked Jasmine.

"Kansas City, Missouri," said Jasmine. "We're pulling out tomorrow, cocker spaniel and all."

"Good luck," said Corinne, absolutely meaning it this time. She hugged them both. "Thank you so much for not inviting me to your wedding," she said in a springy voice.

Both women laughed, but Jasmine said, "It was kind of stupid, because now we've joined our school loans and then made one big mess. But, we're going to kick ass on that mess."

"Have at it," said Corinne. Her debts weren't anywhere as large as those of her friends, but they would still take her years to pay back. Especially since she didn't want to go to Silicon Valley to work. The rents were way too high, the rewards far too low. No, she could hide in a hidey-hole for a while, paying everybody back where rents were rock-bottom. She came from a holler; going back to one didn't bother her, as long as it wasn't the same one.

Tania came over and dragged her and Candace to Sigma Sigma. They had to say goodbye to Mike, an all-around good guy who seemed to have some strange compulsion to help other people move.

He also got a lot of free pizza and beer, so Corinne could see the upside. Sigma Sigma was playing hip hop music, and people were getting half-naked and quite sweaty dancing together.

The girls split up, and Corinne found Mike first. He was in his room, packing his things and sipping from a bottle of beer. The guy had finally gotten a room with a king-sized bed to match his gangly frame, but now he had to leave. Corinne stood next to his bed, and said, "Point to what you want. I know you've got a system."

Mike laughed. "Jeans first," he said, and Corinne knew to pass them over one by one. He put the tops of the jeans in the suitcase, stuck the legs out, then put the next one on going the other way, and folded the legs down. "Where are you going, girl?" Mike asked.

Corinne passed him another pair of jeans ."Some backwoods holler with really good Internet, which I know is kind of a contradiction in terms." Mike laughed. "Those Silicon Valley jobs sound absolutely lovely until you find out their high salaries go entirely toward paying the rent, health and car insurance, and a car that survives the freeway. Shit, been driving hoopties my whole life, and I don't want to change now."

Mike bellowed out another laugh, and Corinne started handing him the dress pants. "Heard you got some good clients," he said quietly. If you wanted to keep a secret, it was a really bad idea to hang around Southern people. They couldn't keep them worth a damn. "Even heard you paid off your smallest loan first."

"Well shit," said Corinne. "Secret's out. I'm paying off the damn loans. I'm still under my parents' health insurance for another year, so that should get me through 'till I can get some for myself."

"Taxes are higher as a self-employed person," said Mike. "I'll take you on as my off-the-book client, help you with an LLC, a limited liability company to you ignorant folk. Open it in Wyoming, where you don't have to pay state taxes."

Corinne said, "You know my number. I'll text you with my new address, and we'll get it done." He nodded. She helped him roll up his dress shirts and put rubber bands around them. "Heard you got job offers to six firms, all over the damn state. I didn't think being a tax attorney paid that damn much, or had that much competition, or are you that good?"

Mike laughed again. "I am," he said, confidently. "Passed the bar my first try, shocked the ever-living hell out of my father." Mike's father, a single dad, drove a bus in St. Louis. Mike had gotten himself scholarships in order to get his degree in tax law. Corinne had shown him how to do jobs on the side as a certified public accountant after he passed the CPA exam, which had paid his way through most of law school.

Corinne asked, "Where are you going to?" It was a hell of a loaded question. Mike was in love with Sam of the basketball scholarship, another tall person, with a shock of black hair, almond eyes, and golden skin. Mike had dreads, short ones, which drove Sam wild and her father insane. Mike and Sam had been debating between Kansas City and St. Louis and had both decided to make decisions that weren't based on each other, so they might end up on opposite sides of the state.

"We both picked St. Louis, and her daddy already took her away before she could go to any parties," he said, quietly. "This is my one and only beer, 'cause I don't feel much like partying without her. Going to follow her down, move in with her when her idiot dad isn't looking."

"Prejudiced idiot," agreed Corinne. "Anyone who looks at your skin color rather than the content of your character hasn't been listening to Martin Luther King." Mike and Corinne bumped fists. Sam was first-generation Chinese, and her father did not want his number one daughter marrying a black man. Mr. Lu was going to be in for one hell of a surprise. Sam and Mike had secretly married the year before, and they were moving in together whether he liked it or not.

"Thank you for picking up and moving all of those easy chairs into the shelter cages, and the sofas in for the big dogs," said Corinne. They moved on to rolling T-shirts and holding their shape with rubber bands.

"Least I could do," said Mike. "Sam picked out one of those little shaky Chihuahuas, and I got me the sweetest little boxer, so have to pick up Hunter and Daisy on the way out of town. Already adopted them, and Panzer's holding them for me. Got to pack this real tight, so their harnesses and beds fit in the SUV. Their cages collapse, but I'll be damned if I'll trap some dog in a cage for the whole trip. They've been in cages for weeks now; time they got out."

Corinne tried desperately not to cry about saying goodbye to Mike. She handed him the last of the t-shirts. "I ain't folding your underwear, man," she said quietly. He choked out a laugh, as the two of them held each other tight. "You tell Sam to hold in there," said Corinne. "Tell her to remember the advice I gave her."

"Her father is trying all that guilt shit," said Mike. "She just smiles an inscrutable smile at him, drives him crazy. He knows damn well she's not listening to a thing he says, so he starts yelling, and she simply walks away. Took him about three times, but now he lowers his voice."

Corinne nodded. "So glad it worked. My parents call about once a year, when they remember they have a daughter. If either one of them tells me how to live my life, I don't talk with them, say I have to get off the phone, do something."

"I'm damn sorry neither one of them were there at graduation. Dad's out there, running some sort of Lego solution to get that SUV filled up. Says he's going to follow me all the way to St Louis, help us get into the new apartment. He loves Sam like she's gold."

"She is," said Corinne. She brushed away a tear, and said, "Ain't no crying, 'cuz we happy. You got yourself a really good job and a real fine woman, and you're getting out of this place." They both laughed a watery laugh. Mike towered over her, kissed her forehead. Corinne slipped out, found Kandace, and drowned her tears with some sort of strawberry drink while Kandace rubbed her back. Kandace left her cooler bag of non-alcoholic drinks under Corinne's legs, and she and Tania went hunting for their own people to say goodbye to.

At the next stop, Corinne was on the non-drinking part of the night, sitting with Kandace getting their toes done at the Sigma Delta Gamma house. She wasn't entirely sure how she got there, but she knew down deep inside she needed to get sober, or she'd end up in a puddle of tears on the floor. Or, throwing up, which was always an elegant solution to her problems. She had the worst goodbye of the night coming up, and needed to face it head-on. Kandace handed her some iced lime concoction, and Corinne drank it down. "How are you holding up?" asked Kandace.

Corinne held up a hand. "Smell the acetone. Look at the pretty colors. Just look at it, silver-blue. I'm going to look like a goddess." Corinne actually somewhat believed that. Her gauzy shirt floated with the fans, and Tania had given her some of her jeweled clips. Her long black hair was pulled back, but the tips still floated in the breeze from the fans. Her blue-black hair was straight at the top and curled on the ends, completely natural, which made other girls crazy. Corinne figured it was a hint of Cherokee in her genes coming out, but deep down, she suspected her blond-haired, blue-eyed father wasn't her actual birth dad. Corinne hadn't confronted her mother yet, mainly because when the woman's lips were moving, she was lying, manipulating, or gaslighting.

Corinne pushed away her negative thoughts with her silver-blue nails, and looked over at Kandace. "You know that Tania is going to want to go over and whale on someone at the Society for Creative Anachronism's Ale Party, don't you?"

Tania glared at Corinne. "Sitting right here, you know, heifer. You know damn well that I can fight."

"Yeah," said Corinne. "We all can. What I don't get is how you and Kandace changed places. Kandace, I had to drag you out of bars because you wanted to knock somebody out on more times than I can think about, and Tania's the one who beats the shit out of people with swords. Don't make no damn sense."

Tania laughed so hard that she doubled over. "Girl, what I don't understand is why you never fought with me."

Corinne thought it over. "I could have, but then I could not have done any volunteering. I had enough trouble finding time to sleep and eat as it was. Besides, kickboxing videos are pretty damn awesome."

"Lazy heifers," said Kandace, making both of them laugh.

They walked out into the night, and Corinne sobered up on the walk. Corinne and Kandace walked over to watch Tania fight, and sat on hay bales. "These things are incredibly uncomfortable," complained Kandace.

"What are we going to do about our girl?" asked Corinne. "Who the hell gave her permission to get a teaching job on the other side of the planet?"

"Wasn't me," said Kandace. The two of them sang the Shaggy song about a man caught red-handed stepping out with someone other than his girlfriend, thereby losing his girl. The rest of the crowd sang the various parts of the song, making all of them laugh.

Corinne took some sort of strawberry thing from Kandace's bag. She opened it, took a sip, and watched Tania beat the snot out of some girl. "Damn, she's good."

"Rely on that," said Kandace. "She's going to be real good no matter what the hell we do. We got to get our shit together, ready for her whenever she comes back."

"What if she doesn't?" asked Corinne.

Kandace snorted, then by way of an answer, started singing Tom Petty's "American Girl." The crowd got into it again, and someone found the song on a cellphone, so they started all over again, this time with Tom Petty's riffs. They finished with a cheer as Tania won, then Tania fought the next fight.

Somehow they ended up getting Tania's stuff and going to a pancake house. Corinne fought not to cry the whole damn time because Tania needed to be happy, because she was starting a new life. The bacon tasted like sawdust in her mouth, but Corinne got strong for her friend.

They ended up at the airport, hugged it out, and left Tania in front of the security gate. Kandace dragged her out when Corinne wanted to stand there and watch Tania go through the line. "She don't need no heifer making moon eyes at her, when all she's trying to do is get the hell out of here." Kandace dragged her out to the truck and said, "Get the hell in. We've got to drive all the way back, get our stuff in our vehicles, and get the hell out of here too."

"I wish we were staying together," said Corinne. "But you've got to go hide out in a cabin again, and I understand why. I really do. But at some point, when you're ready to rejoin the world, I'll be here."

"I know," said Kandace. "That's why I can go do my hiding like that. But, I need to do the Twelve Steps again. You know the quiet writing is when I do the best with it. You know I need to change. I've still got a porcupine under my skin. I'm not like you. I hate people. I can't hear them blather and hug them and tell them that they're going to be okay unless they're another alcoholic."

"Don't go wanting to be me," mourned Corinne. "I ain't got a job, and you and Tania are the only two who know that I only got two offers, and turned them both down. I ain't built for no rat race. I'm a country girl. I'm going to have to live and die based on that."

Kandace said, "I did the damn math with you, and you were right. You wouldn't have made enough to make any dent into your loans, and you would have had to find a roommate situation with six other people just to afford a roof over your head."

"I wish I were Mike. He's got himself two dogs and a woman, and I can't bring any animals with me because I have no idea where I'm going to live."

Kandace shrugged. "Adopt one later. Now, quit your bellyaching, pull up your cell phone, and go through every stinking classified and PennySaver in any small town, looking for a house, apartment, henhouse, or outhouse to live in," she said, mimicking Tommy Lee Jones' line in *The Fugitive.* Corinne laughed, pulled out her cell phone, and began her search.

By the time they got back, it was well past dawn. There was a herd of students leaving. Some were smiling hugely. Many were obviously hungover, and quite a few of them had the wide-eyed look of absolute terror. In the back of the cars, trucks, and SUVs were microwaves, hot plates, clothes, and diplomas.

They found a space around back, parked, and ran up two flights of stairs. They had managed to get a triple; both of them ignored Tania's empty bed. Corinne had the top bunk because Kandace would fall out of the top when she used to get drunk. Corinne opened her bag, checked her packing, made sure she had her diploma and her passport. Tania had made all of them get passports when she decided to go teach in South Korea. Corinne closed up her suitcase, then double-checked the box with her bedding, winter clothes, and shoes.

Corinne's makeup and few pieces of costume jewelry were stowed in her rolling bag. She'd sold everything her parents had given her long before to pay for what her parents didn't cover, which was a great deal. All three of them had cobbled together scholarships, grants, and, in Corinne's case, parental money to get through masters' degrees in five years. Their debts were staggering.

Kandace walked her box to the top of the stairs, finding the elevator crammed with students with their boxes. Corinne took the box, walked it down, opened the back of her ancient hooptie hatch-back, and slid in the back. She closed the hatch, jogged up both flights of stairs, and got her rolling bag. She wrestled the bag back down, managed to get the hatch up, and slid the suitcase right in on its side. The wheel well got in the way, so she slid it back out, opened up the front passenger side, pulled the seat forward, stood the bag upright, put it behind the seat, and slid the seat back. The seat held the bag in place like a vise.

Kandace came down with the microwave, and somehow that slid into the hatch properly. Corinne got the hatch closed, and said, "Can I help you, girlfriend?"

"Already got everything in," said Kandace. They stood and stared at each other, then grabbed each other and held on tight.

They let go, and Corinne said, "I've got my eye on you. Text me with the dates and times of your meetings."

Kandace shook her head. "That's between me and my sponsor. Remember, if I was able to stay sober last night, I'll be fine now."

"Miss you already," said Corinne.

Kandace handed her two colas with little insulated sleeves on them. "With this heat, you'll have to bang these down before they get hot." Corinne laughed, and slid them into the drink holder holes in the console. She slid out of the car and stood up, ready to hug her friend again, but Kandace was already heading toward the corner. Kandace turned, waved, and was gone.

Corinne wiped the tears out of her eyes, got in the hot car, turned on the air conditioner, rolled down the windows to blow out the hot air, popped the top on the first can of Coke, put the first address listed in a PennySaver ad into her cell phone's GPS, and slid it into the holder. She plugged the phone into the cigarette lighter. The first address was two and a half hours away, but at least she had a destination. She pulled out, leaving her old life behind.

# DESTINATION

orinne was completely terrified. Everyone had already rented out their places. In a little place called Broomfield, the little old lady had decided not to rent out a room in her house when her daughter moved in. In Mavenfield, someone had already answered the ad and moved in. So, she zipped down south after consuming a fried chicken sandwich that tasted far better than it should have with fries and a Coke. She got another Coke and kept driving.

Steele Rock was so off the major highway it was actually surprising that the road was paved. There were brick duplexes with flags flying overhead, porches in shades of brown, yellow, gray, and white. There was a Hardee's, the only fast-food for many miles. There was a single Main Street, with a nail shop, barbershop, salon, store that sold boots, clothing stores for men and women, and a feed store, with people in denim going in and out. There was a nursery that sold trees, shrubs, plants, and huge bags of manure. There was a tiny post office, a convenience store, and also some strip malls with a lot of shuttered businesses.

There were railroad tracks and the aptly-named Deep River that flowed through town. The Rock River flowed into it, so there were several bridges in town. One of them was even a covered bridge, painted red with black trim. There was a rainbow-painted barn with a canoe on top near the river. There were farms surrounding the town with fields of corn and soybeans marching in green rows, and hillsides leading to mountains. There were houses clustered on hillsides, and trailers by both rivers, ready to be washed away if the rivers should overflow.

The house in the ad was a small house in white, with bits of gray trim. Corinne figured out where the hell she was supposed to be staying. There was a carport separate from the house, something from the '70s. Over the top was a small apartment, and there was a complete wall at the back of the carport. You couldn't see under it to the pecan and dogwood trees surrounding the house. The lawn was a bright green, with a riot of brightly colored flowers planted all around the outside of the house and down the walkway.

Corinne parked in front of the carport instead of under it, got out, and felt the heat slamming into her body. The crickets sang as if they were going to get some sort of bonus for extra noise. Corinne stretched after having been in the car for nearly three hours, felt her shoulders, neck, and back pop. She turned and walked toward the door, but a woman and a sunny yellow dress and black sandals came streaking across the yard from next door. "Raynelle! Raynelle!" The woman had black hair in numerous braids on one side, and a lovely wave on the other side. She had a crimson as an accent—crimson lips, dragon nails, and toenails.

Raynelle came out, an elderly woman with short, wiry gray hair in a flowered dress that flowed to her knees and black flip-flops. She was short but upright. Her hands were gnarled. "Jana, what in the Savior's name are you going on about?" The woman looked over at Corinne and said, "You-all here about the ad?"

"Yes, ma'am," said Corinne. "I graduated from university yesterday, computer science, and I just need a little house with an internet hookup."

Raynelle looked her up and down. "You know how to work, girl?" She asked. "Not much around here, except working in the feed store.

You looking for insurance or any of that nonsense, ain't going to get it 'round here."

Corinne nodded. "My daddy's going to pay my health insurance for one more year, and I work online. I make websites. Did you need help around here?"

"I'll knock fifty dollars off your rent a month, you clean my house twice a week, help me gardening. Hurts my knees, can't lift those bags of manure no more. You help me, girl, we got ourselves a deal."

Jana said, "She ain't seen the place yet."

Raynelle waved toward the carport house. "Go look in it, girl. Door is open. Don't have much call to lock our doors around here. Ain't nothing much for them to steal anyway. You want what I have that bad; you must need it more than me."

Corinne bobbed her head. "Yes, ma'am." She turned, found a little staircase on the side of her carport, and walked up. Some of the boards were a little loose, and they creaked alarmingly. Corinne whipped out her phone, pulled out her checklist program, and put "Fix stairs" as the first thing on a new list, right under "Get holler apartment." She opened the door and stood there, absolutely stunned. She realized she probably needed to shut the door behind her to prevent mosquitoes from getting in, so she entered quickly.

There was a pink and white Murphy bed that folded out of the wall in the middle of bookshelves on the opposite side from the door. There was a fat chair with an ottoman in a cabbage rose print and a fifteen-year-old television. The apartment smelled of lemon polish. There was a tiny kitchen with the sink, the countertop big enough for a microwave, two small cabinets, and a toaster oven. The refrigerator was a three-quarter size. There was a tiny two-person table that had leaves that could fold up to take two more seats. The two extra seats were in the corner, folded up. There was a bathroom, the door wide open, with a glass shower, and a toilet. The walls were done in happy colors of yellow and light blue. The bathroom had ancient blue tiles, cracked in some places. Corinne pulled out her checklist and added "Replace bathroom tile" to her list.

Corinne decided not to keep the women outside in the heat,

turned around, walked out the door, and down the stairs. She walked right up to the porch, nodded to Jana and Raynelle, and said, "Ma'am, I'll take it. I'm sorry, ma'am, but I only have a month's rent right now. I can get you the other month in two weeks, depending on when next month's rent is due. Is it due on the last day of the month? Maybe on the 28th because that's the same for all the months?"

Jana looked at Corinne. "You got cash?" she asked.

"You got an ATM?" countered Corinne. "I saw the little bank, and the little glass ATM, if you've got a closer one, I'll go there.

"No, ma'am, we only got the Countyline One Bank," said Raynelle.

"I'll be back in about fifteen minutes, ma'am," said Corinne. "Do you need anything from the store?"

"Bring me a jar of crunchy peanut butter," said Raynelle. "And some of them Hershey's Kisses, if you can find them. They may be at the convenience store instead of the regular store. You do that; you'll get peanut butter cookies with the chicken and biscuits. I also got peaches and green beans."

"Yes, ma'am," said Corinne. She turned to get back in the car, then turned back. "I apologize. I do not know where my manners went. My name is Corinne. I'll be right back with your money, ma'am." Raynelle nodded at her, and Jada had her mouth open like a fish.

Corinne smiled at them both, turned around, and marched right back to her car. She got in and headed out as a sedate speed to the bank, the store, and the convenience store, which were all less than a block away from each other.

She came back with the groceries, handed the money over in a bank envelope, and said, "Just holler out the door if you need me. I'm going to be moving in. Do you have cleaning supplies I can use, ma'am?"

"There is a mop, bucket, and broom upstairs in the cleaning closet," said Raynelle. Jada had gone back next door.

Corinne took the time to clean her apartment first, having picked up gloves, washable rags, and blue cleaning spray at the store. She sprayed everything, swept, and mopped the floor with the ancient broom and mop she found in a tiny closet at the end of the kitchen.

The broom looked like it would fall into toothpicks at any moment. She cleaned every surface, then brought up her box, then her rolling bag, then the microwave oven. She put the microwave on the clean but ancient counter next to the two-burner ancient stove, plugged it in, and input the correct time.

Corinne grabbed her tape measure, went back outside, and measured the planks on the stairs. She went up and down them several times to be sure which ones had a problem, then went to the lumber store. She found scrap lumber, had them pre-drilled for the bolts, bought a wrench, bolts, and nuts, and replaced the three steps. This time, she parked under the carport.

She went back up, washed her hands, and smiled when she heard a whistle. She went back down, crossed the concrete drive over to the house, and was assailed with the beautiful smell of fried chicken.

"If you don't mind being eaten up, it's really nice out on the porch," said Raynelle, referring to the mosquitoes.

"Sounds good," said Corinne. Corinne had a bottle of insect repellent on her at all times and burned citronella candles in her home; Missouri mosquitos were legendary. Raynelle's kitchen was small, with ancient almond-colored appliances, but it was painted a bright yellow, and spotlessly clean. Corinne took the preloaded plates of fried chicken, biscuits cut in half with butter soaking in, and green beans outside and put them on the little tables next to the deck chairs on the front porch. Corinne went back in to get the two jelly jars full of lemonade, and the two napkins. She brought those out as well, then went back in and said, "Anything else I can help you with?" The peanut butter cookies had little Hershey's Kisses nestled in each one of them and were cooling on a rack.

Raynelle washed her hands. "Let's go out." They went out to the porch, sat down, and Raynelle bowed her head. Corinne bowed her head as well, and Raynelle said, "The good Lord done give us fellowship, food on the table, and new friends." Raynelle's strong voice shook a little bit. "The Good Lord done kept the wolf from the door for one more day. In the name of Jesus Christ, Amen."

"Amen," said Corinne. Corinne followed Raynelle's movements, from putting the napkin and her lap, to eating the chicken first. The biscuits had honey and butter and tasted amazing. The green beans were raw and tasted green and fresh. "Ma'am, this is the first home-cooked meal I've had since I went to my friend Tania's grandmother's house." That was a complete horror story, so Corinne closed her mouth on that part.

"I'm glad it's to your liking," said Raynelle. "I was going to ask whether or not you like that kinda cookin', but you done ate two pieces of chicken, and even ate the green beans before you finished your biscuit." Raynelle ate slowly, like old women everywhere. Corinne was exhausted and sat there relaxing on the Adirondack chair. "You get your apartment the way you like it?" Raynelle asked.

"It's perfect for me. I found the Internet hookups, but I haven't plugged anything yet."

"We get a good storm; you won't be gettin' nothin'. You gotta pay me ten dollars extra for the cable bill."

"I can do that."

Raynelle finished her meal. "We put the scraps in the scrap box, behind the sink. I got me one of those tiny dishwashers. Rinse the dishes and put them in there. Then, I'll thank you kindly to go in and bring out four of them cookies. You can have one more if you want, but I only eat two."

"Yes, ma'am." Corinne took the plates, scraped them off into the scrap box, and put them in the tiny dishwasher that sat on the counter. She put four cookies on a plate, and brought out the pitcher of lemonade. She refreshed both glasses, put the plate down, then put the lemonade back in the refrigerator. She sat down and bit into a cookie that made her swoon with delight.

"Why did you come all the way out here?" asked Raynelle. "This be the butt end of nowhere."

Corinne laughed. "I got me some job offers, both of them in cities so expensive the people that make a half-million dollars working ninety hours a week can't afford their own place. I would have been living out of my car in a week. This way, I get to live in a holler like I'm used to, eat the food I like, see the kind of people I like. My parents live in one of those nice duplexes like you've got down near Main Street, owned the thing, my father had a good job. We ate just fine and had a roof over our heads. They moved out and up later on. You could say that we did well. Places like this suit me the best, and I've got bills to pay. I need someplace nice and quiet to build my websites, take some pictures all around here of some pretty things, sell the pictures too."

"You can make a living doing that, just stuff on a computer? I didn't see no camera equipment," she said, admitting that she had been watching Corinne move in.

"I just have a special lens for my phone," said Corinne. "It's good enough for most stuff. And, I already paid off my smallest school loan before I even graduated. My friend Tania says to live low, pay high."

"Sounds like real good words," said Raynelle. "About time for my show. Do you want to watch some Alex Trebek with me?"

Corinne nodded, "I like *Jeopardy*." They went on in, lemonades in hand, and Corinne smiled when she noticed the elderly woman's flat screen TV. They sat down in the big black dual recliners, and watched TV, calling out the answers, making each other laugh.

# FITTING IN

*C*orinne struggled not to hit anything. Instead, she took off her headphones, slid them in their case, and zipped it shut. She unhooked the power cable from the laptop, rolled it up, and put it where it belonged in the laptop bag. Then, she unhooked the offending Internet cable, closed the laptop, and slid into its case. She turned off the air conditioning but left the fan running. She had to get out of the stifling heat anyway. Her air conditioner trickled rather than spitting out cold air.

Corinne traipsed down the stairs to her vehicle, opened the door, and slid the laptop bag over the back of her seat and into the webbing. The air was so moist that she felt her skin being moisturized and sizzled at the same time. Corinne sat down on the beach towel she had across the front seat, slid on her driving gloves, and turned on the car, leaving the door wide open and the air conditioner on full. She closed the door when the air conditioner started spitting out something of a lower temperature, and she backed out.

She took River Road to Main Street and saw that the river was low. She put it in her head as a conversation topic and crawled down Main Street. The cable didn't work at her little carport apartment, and she needed to complete work if she wanted to get paid. She parked and charged up the car at the little charging station where they sold gas as well.

She grabbed her laptop case, slung it over her shoulder, left her driving gloves in the car, and crossed the street to the diner. Corinne nearly collapsed at the wave of cold air that hit her. She walked right up to the back booth on the left and faced the wall. There was a plug under the table for what used to be tabletop jukeboxes, and she put her strip down, then plugged in the laptop.

Corinne slapped two dollars for the first round down on the counter, and Dana came up with the first Coke of the day. No ice, no glass, just the sweating can of Coke. "No internet in your apartment again?" Dana asked. "Must be a pain in the ass." Dana had long red hair caught up in a clip. She wore a simple black jean skirt and a black sleeveless t-shirt with a rose design printed on it. She had a long face and a jutting jaw, and her glasses had wire rims with a pink tint. She was fast, precise, and loved her customers.

Corinne took her headphones, a pencil and a pad of paper for the bizarre ideas that would enter her head, and the plastic tray on its spindly legs she sat on her lap out of the case. Corinne was able to do this because the diner's table wasn't bolted to the floor like tables in other coffee shops and could be pushed back. Corinne kicked off her shoes, threw the towel on to the other side and straightened it out with her feet, propped her feet up, and grimaced at Dana. "Sorry to be taking up a booth again. But, you know you've got the best air conditioner and Coke in the entire county."

Dana laughed. "That we do. Tell you about the pie later?"

Corinne groaned. "You're going to make me as fat as a heifer." Dana laughed. Corinne put in her earphones, her signal that she needed to start work.

Dana nodded, smiled, and went back to pour coffee at the counter for Jude Hardesty, the police chief, finishing off the last of his eggs. Jude bent his head of dark, curly, short hair over his cell phone, poking at it with fingers that matched the cinnamon he liked in his coffee. The man liked to read books while eating, mostly science fiction. He ate keto, so no biscuits, pancakes, or waffles for him.

Stella Meineke was in the back booth, checking all the accounts for her lumber business on her cell phone while she finished her last cup of coffee. Her blonde, shoulder-length hair was going gray. She had corded muscles, wrinkles around her eyes and mouth, and skin tanned from the sun. Dana knew better than to bother one of her favorite customers. Stella realized she was there and waved Dana over. "You tell Corinne there when she comes up for air that I got plenty of scraps for her, hear?"

"I will," said Dana. Becoming the messenger service for Corinne meant Dana was raking in the dollars. They knew damn well she wouldn't pass on a message unless they tipped her at least a dollar, none of that quarter crap. Corinne had made it her mission to make sure her elderly landlord had good railings, no squeaky floorboards in her house, and had even patched the roof early one morning. Stella Meineke was making money in dribs and drabs off Corinne, but it was constant. More constant than being the overflow when area home builders ran out of lumber from the large home stores. Corinne's work had guilted more than one family member to come in and start working on the houses of their elderly parents, aunts, uncles, and cousins. And, in Raydon County, you tended to have a lot of cousins.

Corinne didn't notice when the diner emptied out, seven out of the eight booths and all six stools empty. Dana cleaned everything, filled everything up, then pulled up the used laptop Corinne had bought for her and called it a tip. Dana pulled up a free website called Free Code Camp and started telling the world hello while learning how to code like Corinne, her new hero. Dana's father Jack cleaned the grill, checked the refrigerators to be sure he hadn't run out of bacon, had a cigarette out back then came back in, washed his hands, and worked on the bills in the office.

Corinne had two different websites in the testing phase after getting the number of pages they needed, colors to look right, and most of the buttons sized and colored correctly. Now, each link had to go to the correct place. Internet advertising didn't work, unless the person pressing *Buy Now* or *Visit Website* actually went to the right place. Once all of that was done, Corinne had the long, hard slog to get the pages to say exactly what they needed to say.

Corinne went through first one Coke, then two, then she had loaded fries with cheddar, bacon, and sour cream, a departure from her usual piece of apple pie. First one website, then the other, were hammered into obeying Corinne's directives. Neither one was quite ready to turn over to the clients yet, but they were getting there. Corinne sipped a Coke with one hand while typing with the other and talking on her earphones, using a special speaking program that allowed her to move around verbally on her computer. Corinne's ADD allowed her to keep track of all of it.

Corinne came up for air, took off her headphones, stretched, and heard the clink of glasses, silverware, and plates. She looked around and was stunned to find a full diner. She shut down her computer, pushed everything off to the side, changed seats to the opposite half of the booth, because even Corinne knew it was incredibly rude to eat without letting someone see your eyes. Dana came scooting over. "Today we've got meatloaf, and a Caesar salad with my daddy's superior grilled chicken."

"Caesar salad, and water this time, and the apple pie with cinnamon ice cream for dessert." Corinne stretched, hearing bones pop.

"On it," said Dana. "Meineke says she's looking forward to your coming back because she has a load of scrap lumber you can play with." Corinne nodded. She was used to Dana being the spokesperson for the entire town at that point. "I'll bring you a nice chocolate Coke when you go back to work." Dana hustled off, happy that one more hungry diner had been taken care of.

Five minutes later, Vern came in, found all the tables filled, every seat at the bar taken. A lot of people's air conditioners were on the fritz, and absolutely no one in their right mind wanted to cook in that heat. He cut his eyes to Corinne, and she nodded her head and broke down her rig so that he could sit and Dana could put his plates on the table. She put her feet on the floor and smiled. "What's going on,

Vern?" she asked, as she shrugged her shoulders and stretched her spine.

"Rivers are getting low in this heat," said Vern. Vern ran the multi-colored Rainbow Canoe Shack down by Rock River. It was named for the arrowheads people found in it; it was actually wide and meandering. It was a favorite summer pastime to take canoes, inner tubes, and rafts up the river. His patrons would float back down, have Vern put the flotation devices back on the roof of his van, and then Vern drove everyone back up the river to do it all over again. Vern also rented out safety vests, sold towels and sunscreen, and made a good living. In the winters, he built canoes the old way, by hand. Vern, a reservation escapee, had the last name of Running Deer. He was married to Mary Lou Chambers, a local former cheerleader and a whiz with tax accounting for farms. Vern had graying hair with wild curls on top, with a beard and mustache. He had ropy arms from all the rowing and portage, his skin nut-brown and wrinkled from the sun.

"I saw the rivers were low, coming in. I've got websites to finish, Vern. We get some rain, and I get paid, two days later, I'll be knocking down your door," Corinne promised.

"Those people asking for a lot of web pages? Must be big city people. I just need our landing page, or booking page, and a coupon landing page if we're running those things. Most of us can do with two or three pages. Less, if it's just informational, like the company's address and phone number, and what you do."

Dana came up. "I got a Reuben for you, coffee, and cherry pie, unless you want something different," Dana said to Vern.

"Sounds good. You hear about the silly city slickers ordering all sorts of web pages?" he said, speaking to Dana, gesturing to Corinne. "Idiots."

"Hey. Be nice to my idiots. They're going to pay for charging my car, my rent, and my car insurance." Corinne had paid to have the hooptie converted to electric, saving her a fortune in gasoline. Dana laughed and went to go put in the order.

Vern shook his head. "Girl, you hauling a lot of stuff anywhere?"

Corinne shook her head. "Just this," she said, gesturing to her computer bag.

"Then you're an idiot, girl. Scooters and motorcycles have a lot lower insurance rates, you can fill them up for a lot less and run them all month without having to fill up, unless you're road tripping, or get one of them electric conversions. You'll have to get yourself a summer weight jacket and motorcycle boots and wear your jeans when you're out. Get yourself a helmet. There's this guy named Mitch. We call him the Harley guy around here. His brother James is a hiking and fishing guide, works all around here," said Vern, waving his finger around to denote the surrounding territory. "Those guys work a lot of days in a row, then get a lot of days off. Mitch refinishes dead bikes, makes the run again. Builds some of 'em from scratch. Plenty of them are sized for someone like you."

"I don't have a motorcycle license."

"That Mitch guy, he'll train you, take you for the test. Says it's a pain in the ass, so many unlicensed people are riding bikes through his damn hills." Vern guffawed. "His brother James thinks he owns half the county, on account of he works all over these mountains, and they got state parks that touch each other around here. Makes for great hiking and camping. And those people visit me, 'cause he tells 'em about my business, and so I'm happy." He took a sip of his coffee. "Problem is, you'll have to park it come winter. But you ain't got a four-wheel drive anyhow, have to park that as well or get yourself killed. I make a little extra, ferrying people around in winter in my Jeep. I can get you back and forth here, long as there's not a blizzard."

"Sounds like a plan." Corinne had never thought of herself as a Harley girl before. It intrigued her.

Their food came, and both of them were silent as they devoured it. They ate their pie, because no one in their right mind messed with the Sunshine Diner's pie. "I take it you need to finish with your current clients?" Vern asked Corinne.

"Then, get paid. Once I get each segment of the website back to them, I get another chunk. They want revisions, they get one check-list, one more pass, then the last chunk." Corinne tilted her head. "Give me a week. Then, I need a motorcycle license before I buy the bike. Maybe set up an appointment, get me riding."

Vern poked at his phone, sent a virtual card to her. He took out his wallet to pay the check and gave a slow smile when Corinne sent a text to Mitch. Corinne also paid up to her current point, including for the chocolate Coke Dana brought after taking the plates off the table. Vern tipped an imaginary hat and left.

Corinne washed up and slammed out one of the web sites. She stood up and did a little happy dance in the now-empty restaurant, making Dana laugh. Corinne changed to apple juice, double-checked everything, every link, every line, and sent the website to the client. She did another happy dance, paid Dana, broke down her rig again, and checked her phone. Mitch had sent a text. *Off in four days. Will train you and show you bikes that I have for females. Must have a license to buy.*

Corinne texted back. *Sounds good. I agree.* She stood, shouldered her bag, and went out to her baking car to be home in time for her landlord's country dinner.

~

*H*itting up the hardware store after a dinner of fried chicken, corn on the cob, biscuits, and homemade sun tea from a giant jar had seemed like a good idea. But, Corinne was moving like a sloth with the weight of dinner in her stomach. At this rate, she'd be done when the stars shone.

She found Stella at the cash register. After work hours, which was after seven in the country, meant there was a line. One was a wrinkled woman with wiry steel-gray hair in jeans, steel-toed boots, and a cowboy hat purchasing what seemed like glass jars of every kind of nail and screw. Corinne assumed she was a contractor or a handyperson, or maybe house flipper who bought and renovated houses then sold them. A young man, barely eighteen, weedy, with pimples, bought a scary-looking nail gun and enough nails to build a barn. A tallish man with his short hair under a blue ball cap and dark eyes that looked like melted chocolate had a coil of rope over his shoulder. His blue sleeveless shirt did nothing to hide his muscles. *Hubba hubba,* Corinne thought.

Stella saw Corinne and pointed at the back. There was a pile of scrap in back with the tips sprayed orange with washable paint. Corinne nodded, not interrupting Stella chatting with the contractor woman. "Yellin house, Mabel?" Stella asked.

"Yep. Roof and porches are disaster areas. Demo tomorrow." Stella nodded as if Mabel had told her the secret of life and the universe.

Corinne pulled on her gloves and shoved her way out the back door. Her scrap was in a little pile, hidden behind a box. Corinne grinned; Stella had her back. Corinne quickly came up with a price, then hauled the wood around to her hatchback. She managed to jigsaw-puzzle the wood in. She went back in, stood in line, paid Stella. The hubba-hubba guy was long gone. Pity. She went home to piece together a lattice for Raynelle's roses. Corinne wanted to give back. The internet wasn't Raynelle's fault; poorly placed underground lines were, and Corinne's phone wouldn't work as a web connection there. So, bit by bit, she paid Raynelle back for her kindness.

# INTERMINABLE WAIT

*C*orinne's first bike ride was up and down Mitch's long driveway. Mitch wore jeans, a t-shirt that had a wolf on a motorcycle, and a do-rag holding back his shaggy brown hair. He had ripped muscles on his arms and looked as if he could bench press the bikes he sold. His hair curled on his shoulders and had a barely-there mustache and goatee. He wore heavy motorcycle boots, even in the heat. The heat didn't seem to disturb him at all, while Corinne sweated under the lightweight motorcycle jacket he made her wear just to look at the Harleys. Corinne had bought some motorcycle boots online and was stunned when they fit perfectly. She also bought motorcycle gloves with reinforced Kevlar knuckles, and a bright red helmet with a mic so she could talk to others while on the bike. Mitch had nodded when she put them on.

Corinne didn't have to think about the bike she wanted. Mitch has a used 2006 Harley Davidson Softail Deluxe in red with miles of chrome. It was, however, well out of her price range. She sighed, and shook her head. "You've done a beautiful job with her, but I just don't have that kind of money."

Mitch nodded. "We can do some trades. I hear you sell custom websites."

"Mine are not cheap. Fifteen hundred dollars for a small business with one complete reworking and going live. Three thousand for the whole deal. That includes hooking up to online payment services, which also takes point of service credit cards if you sell a bike here, with pictures, video uploads, sales landing pages, all the things you need to do to run an online business. Connects to whatever shipping service you need, from pickup to delivery. Even assigns a tracking number right then."

"I'll take two. The big ones, all the bells and whistles. I hear you got enough cash for the rest when you're done with your current clients. That works for you?"

"We will need to sign some contracts to cover our butts on both ends, but hell yeah, we've got a deal," said Corinne. They shook on it.

"Let's get you trained first. Then we can sign some contracts inside, and I happen to know that there is a case of Coke in my refrigerator. I even have Mountain Dew, the yellow kind, not the back holler kind." People in the backwoods still made moonshine, otherwise known as mountain dew, a liquor with enormous amounts of alcohol.

"Bring it on." Mitch showed Corinne every part of the bike, quizzed her at every turn, making her feel like she was back in school again. He went over every aspect of motorcycle law with a clipboard, told her facts and relentlessly quizzed her. He used his own bike, another Harley Softail in black, and had her sit in front of him as he rode.

Mitch lived in an A-frame house perched on a hillside. He pointed in three different directions as they rode down his winding paved road to the mountain road. "My brother James works here, there, and over there," he said. "He's a fishing, camping, and hiking guide, cross-country skiing and ice fishing in winter. Works nearly constantly with kind of random days off during his busy season. His job keeps poachers off the land, keeps hikers hiking trails with enough water to go the distance."

Mitch showed her the water he kept in his jacket, with a straw embedded in the lid so he could sip. "Put water in this thing, stick it in the freezer. Do two or three, you have nice cold water, and your own refrigeration units. I have a cooling jacket, and I can sell you one. Global warming is not a joke. Dehydration can kill you dead, and so can heat stroke, especially wearing the leathers we wear, vented or not."

"I hear you," said Corinne, the microphone feeling comfortable to her, his voice reassuring in her ears.

Mitch showed her how to accelerate, decelerate, lean, stop, and turn around. He then had her ride her new bike with him on the back, and do everything he had done. Corinne made it all the way to the end, then turned back around to head back up. She parked a little sideways, but got everything back where it needed to go. Mitch handed her a water pouch, and made her drain it. He gave her another half-frozen one to put in her jacket, and had her check out her new bike. They rode up and down the driveway again, first with him riding behind her, then with him following her. He relentlessly quizzed her about the parts of the bike, the law, what to do if an animal crosses your path, and other situations like that. Then, he took her out on the winding mountain road, and they went up for about twenty minutes, then turned around and came back.

Corinne had no idea why she wasn't terrified. She felt exhilarated, very conscious of every decision she made, very willing to learn. The only thing that scared her was making a mistake. She hated making mistakes. She thought of herself as a blank canvas that Mitch was painting.

They put their helmets under the seats of their respective bikes, then went inside Mitch's A-frame and stripped off their leathers and boots. When she looked up, Corinne was stunned by the beautiful space. The living room was to the right, with a rounded couch in front of a fireplace hanging from the ceiling. There was a flat-screen TV on a stand, and gaming consoles underneath, in front of a black couch with reclining seats on each end off to the side. There was a floating staircase leading up to what were obviously bedrooms. There were desks against the wall, with double screens with black leather computer chairs in front of them. Mitch walked past all of that to the galley kitchen, against the opposite wall. Corinne had to force herself to take steps inside, her head still on swivel. The entire back wall was made of panels of glass that showed the surrounding mountains in smoky blue, purple, brown, green, and strips of red and white. She closed the door behind her and went to look out the windows, stunned by the view.

Mitch handed her a Mountain Dew, and she popped the top. "Let's go to the computers," said Mitch. "We'll get these contracts out of the way, you can pay me what you can, and we can talk about how you're getting that test taken so I can get that awful hatchback off your hands."

Corinne actively focused on Mitch. "I know it's a hooptie, but I was a college student. What can I say?"

Mitch nodded. "We've got teenagers all over these mountains who are real tired of driving their daddy's truck. They'd be willing to take a piece of shit like that, help you pay me a little more cash upfront. Besides, it's electric, so you get some extra for teens not having to stop to fill up on gas."

Corinne nodded as they walked across the floor. She couldn't help it; she stopped and stared out the wall of glass. "Where are the best trails?"

Mitch pointed off into the distance to the left. "You live right about there, in what we call the Bottoms. You can't see that part of town from here, because it's in a holler. But, it's there. Now, over to the far left is some really good hiking. Not too strenuous, some rivers and waterfalls, but you got to stay on the main path."

"I take it there are animals? I've seen every kind of bird imaginable, squirrels, deer, chipmunks, raccoons. We've got to keep our trash locked down tight in my holler." Raccoons were highly intelligent and tended to get into people's trash unless one locked the bins.

Mitch grinned. "There are goat paths, and yes, actual goats. Sheep too. Wolves, bobcats, foxes, bears, but mostly the small black ones. Cougars. We have one, at least. My brother's been tracking her for a while. Rabbit, deer, that sort of wildlife. I would suggest you carry bear spray, and if you see a wolf or bear, just back away. Don't draw attention to yourself. We've got springs up there, and even with global warming, most of the animals are getting enough to drink and eat. The wolves have enough to eat without looking to eat you. Our cougar will leave you the hell alone. My brother says he needs to find the exact radius of her territory, protect her from whatever idiots may be up there hunting illegally. Also, if you go hiking, you have to wear orange. Bright orange, the kind you can see from orbit."

That made her laugh. Mitch gestured with his soda can. "Most of our hunters have licenses and aren't blind as bats. But, there's occasionally some drunken idiot who decides to take potshots at hikers. But if any of those idiots do that on government land, hunting out of season, doing anything they shouldn't, they know my brother James will set the law on them. The sheriff will come down on them like a ton of bricks, even if he has known their mamas and daddies for decades."

Corinne made her way over to the computer desks, and sat down on the one on the right. She wiggled the mouse, and it booted right up. She entered into her online drive, and showed Mitch her standard contract. "What's your last name?" she asked.

"Weston. Mitchell Weston. That's for the first contract. You know what I do with the bikes, and my brother James does it too sometimes. It's why we have a couple of bikes to choose from, and why I had something small and pretty enough for you to ride. The next one is for Rachael Camber. There's a really big farm; our land kind of touches it. They grow a lot of heirloom things, heavy believers in crop diversity. The website's a mess. Created it with some website builder, and it just doesn't work for them, and not a coder in the bunch. Rachael writes gardening books too, and has a mess of other businesses. Good luck with that one. You'll do a lot less work with me and a whole lot more work with her. Work on mine first, because she can't work on seventeen things at the same time. Do hers later."

Mitch amended his own contract for the bike, counting the website work as part of the sales price, and allowing her to pay less cash in exchange for letting Mitch sell the car once Corinne had passed the motorcycle license exam. They negotiated numbers, signed the contracts, then Mitch asked her to stay for lunch. Corinne shook her head. "The Internet went wonky at the house again, and getting anyone to fix it involves sacrificing a chicken at the full moon. Was going down to the diner."

Mitch laughed. "Eat a sandwich here, pound out whatever you do on the computer you just used, and there's twelve-packs of both kinds of caffeine you like in the fridge. The other one's my brother James' computer. I'm going to work on another bike after lunch, another one for females. I think there's a market here I haven't tapped into."

Corinne sighed. "You just saved me from getting really fat because of the pie. No one can resist the pie."

Mitch laughed again, padded to the kitchen. Corinne followed him. "I've got turkey, ham, pulled pork, and smoked chicken."

Corinne mock-glared at him. "Why the hell would you bring up anything else when you have pulled pork in your refrigerator?"

Mitch snorted, and took out the pulled pork, hamburger buns, sliced pickles, a sweet barbecue sauce, tomatoes, and stone-ground mustard. He sliced the heirloom tomatoes with ruthless efficiency, shook some salt over them, and built his sandwich. Corinne built hers, heavy on pickles and mustard. She was delighted when Mitch came out with a huge bag of Cool Ranch Doritos. They divvied up the bag and sat at the kitchen table. They concentrated on the food, after Corinne's first moan. "We got a smoker out back, can get you ribs, pulled pork, and smoked chicken whenever you want."

Corinne narrowed her eyes at him. "Once I get more of my school loans paid off, I'm going to have you deliver once a week."

"Hell I will. Come and get it your damn self." They bumped fists, then finished lunch.

Once she finished helping Mitch clean up, Corinne two-fisted, a Coke in one hand, a Mountain Dew in another. Mitch and James had their computers hooked into double screens hanging on the walls. She could not give up this chance to use two screens. She knew damn well she needed to buy two or even three, but with the Internet connection going out so often, it just seemed pointless.

Corinne worked on her second client's site, fixed broken links and made things work as they should. It was a virtual currency site, something she'd never tried to do before. They were APIs connected to real-time trading data on other websites, buttons to buy and trade online currencies like Bitcoin, services to track data, and the liked all being sold at once. There was a forum for traders and links to numerous social media websites. The website was a pain in the ass, and every single part had to look new, exciting, a place digital currency traders would want to visit. She had finally checked every link, done everything that the client asked her to do. She sent an email to her client, asking the client's marketing team to check over every aspect of the website before it went live.

Corinne sat there, dazed, and finished off the Coke. She could smell Mitch before she saw him, and he stood away from her. "Sorry, I smell like a horse right now."

"Like a horse covered in motor oil," Corinne pointed out.

Mitch laughed, then peered at the double screens. "That has got to be the most complex website I've ever seen."

"And I built it from scratch and got it to them early," boasted Corinne. "Thanks to your screens here. It's kind of pointless buying them for myself when the web just doesn't work in my house half the time." She laughed. "I should have charged them double, but after all the add-ons, it's nearly that. At least one and a half times my normal rate."

"Now, I'm sad I cut you a break."

Corinne snorted and pulled up the other site she had completed the few days before and put it up on the other screen. "This is more like what you're looking for. This guy sells antique metal things, like coins and weapons. He needs to show the coins and weapons from all sides, the provenance, and his prices unless he's willing to negotiate. He has little videos about each one, which is just pictures with a slideshow. He just puts in his pictures and some text, and the program automatically, seamlessly inserts the videos into his website. Now it's super-easy to navigate for buyers, and easy for him to load what he's selling." Corinne sighed. "I had to explain that if he has Confederate, Nazi, or other merchandise on his website, he needs to say so and have pictures that don't offend the public. Guy's an introvert, doesn't understand offending people."

"Lots of people around here may have antiques they actually want to sell to him. Farmers dig up their land, find old coins, belt buckles, all that stuff." Mitch stood back from her, afraid of offending her with his scent.

Corinne clicked on the *Want to Sell* button, and a page popped up with instructions on how to take photos, an explanation of how to prove provenance, and how to calculate the desired amount. "This thing even hooks into the shipping service, so when he and whomever wants to sell to him agree on a price, someone will show up from the shipping company with the right kind of box and wrapping. They will even take pictures of it before it is sealed. You get half up front, half when it arrives. Some people around here would earn extra money if they didn't want to donate whatever it is to a museum." Corinne looked over her shoulder at Mitch, whose long hair was stuck to his body with sweat. "You look like a half-drowned horse."

"Stuck my head under the hose, and shook myself out like a dog. You should try it sometime."

She laughed and held up her hands. "Water and electronics do not mix."

"I'm here for two more days, before I take a road trip to drop off a bike." Mitch pointed to his flatbed truck, parked off to the side. "If you can't get online, I don't have a problem with you working here. You're right. That last website would cut it, if it were more badass." Corinne choked out a laugh. "If working here makes you get all of our websites up faster, more power to you. But I have to be here to let you in and out, because it's not just me, my brother James lives here too. And James would absolutely, positively murder me very slowly over several days if I let people he didn't know get in and out of the house with a key without his meeting them first."

Corinne stood, made sure both cans were empty, went to the sink to rinse them and throw them in the recycling, then walked back. "I would not want to be the cause of brotherly dismemberment. Tell you what, I'll text you and see if you're here if I can't get online. Deal?"

"Deal," he said. They bumped fists. He walked her out, and Corinne looked longingly at her new bike, but she couldn't take the exam until Saturday. She opened the door to air out her ancient car, turned on the air conditioner, put on her driving gloves, and waved goodbye.

# TESTING

*C*orinne spent the day in bed after she got both websites rewritten. She had to put off the motorcycle test because, to her stunned surprise, both of the website redos were extensive. She had to charge both of them more than usual because she had to rewrite entire pages. She frankly thought both of them were rearranging deck chairs as opposed to making changes that would actually change sales figures, but if clients wanted to spend extra money, she wasn't going to argue with them. They changed colors, fonts, buttons, button placements, and the content of entire pages. She charged them a lot of money, spent nearly a week making the changes, then took another day to lay in bed.

She thought about studying her motorcycle rule book, but Mitch did that for her by calling her once a day and quizzing her mercilessly. She looked forward to taking the test the very next day, but she knew she would never pass if she was a limp noodle. She bought pulled pork and sandwich fixings from Mitch when he let her use his house to beat on these two websites, so she had food. She also had toaster pastries, and maneuvered herself out of bed to chew on them. She washed them down with a glass of orange juice, stumbled into the shower, and made it to her brand new television, actually a monitor attached to her computer. She pulled up some nonsensical YouTube videos and lay back to watch.

Her phone pinged, and Malcolm texted her. *Hear you've got hiking where you are,* it said.

*I do,* she said.

*Pinged you. Be there in twelve hours.*

Corinne tried texting and calling him, but his phone was dead. That was how Malcolm did things. He showed up, they had a good time, then he disappeared. He enjoyed sex, and so did she, but Corinne knew damn well Malcolm had no interest in any actual responsibilities. It was his way. He had gotten a job in Boston. Corinne wondered if it had worked out, or if he simply took time off to indulge in his yen for hiking. Since there was no way to tell, Corinne just groaned and took a nap.

Corinne woke up, fixed herself a pulled pork sandwich with Cool Ranch Doritos and a Coke on the side, and looked up the local hiking trails online. One trail led to a pool surrounded by rocks, where you could swim din the heat. Another led to a cleft waterfall. There was a cave, but neither one of them were spelunkers, so she marked that one off her list. She packed her backpack with her tarp, rope, carabiners, bear and insect repellents, a whistle, a plastic bag with matches, a blanket, and more. She found her hiking boots and put them by the door, along with her climbing things, lightweight long pants, a short sleeved t-shirt, and the required bright orange vest to put over her head to make her noticeable to hunters. She printed off several maps, remembered to pack her food bars, froze several of her refillable water packs, then took another nap.

Corinne woke up, showered, studied for her exam, and was glad she did when Mitch called. Mitch quizzed her mercilessly, wished her well, and hung up.

Half an hour later, Malcolm showed up, tanned so deeply that his green eyes stood out in his face, with bags of cold Taco Bell, which they reheated in the microwave. He had cut his long black hair short, and still had that carefree smile. He was full of stories of backpacking through the Grand Canyon, a wild weekend in Boston with his new boss at the app company, and a whitewater rafting trip.

He seemed ready to restart his friends-with-benefits relationship. Corinne sighed, but she couldn't resist those green eyes. Their kisses went deeper and deeper, his hand clasped hers. It wasn't that she didn't have a box of condoms. She did, in her dresser drawer, because, as Kandace always said, you never know when you're going to run across a random. But she never thought she'd see Malcolm again. So full of stories, brimming with life, always ready with another tale to make her laugh. She loved his bright-eyed enthusiasm. Corinne had gone on many road trips with Malcolm on those post-exam weekends when she literally could not study anymore. Malcolm Kruger was always doing that, off to traverse some ravine or find some hidden waterfall. She decided to talk to him about canoeing or white water rafting, but he stole her words with his kisses, stroked her with his long fingers.

She woke up at three in the morning, confused. Then she moved, realized she was a bit sore, then remembered why. She laughed a little, deep in her throat, and knew that Malcolm would be grasping for her at four in the morning if she didn't move. She stumbled into the bathroom, cleaned herself up, fell onto the couch, and slipped her cell phone under her pillow. She was asleep a moment later.

Corinne was up before the sun cracked the horizon. She quickly showered, grabbed a Mountain Dew out of the refrigerator, grabbed another one and slid it into her jacket pocket, got on her riding clothes, and walked in her socks down to the carport. She put on her boots on the bottom stair. Mitch came up on her bike, grinning like he was the one taking the test. Corinne finished her Mountain Dew, put on her headset and helmet, and celebrated that this would be the last time that anyone else would drive her bike.

The testing facility was as ugly as government buildings could get, a pink stucco building, although it was nowhere near the Southwest. Corinne strode into the DMV, got in the motorcycle line, and took the exam. She didn't even think about it. Mitch had been quizzing her so much that it seemed to be just another one of Mitch's list of questions.

She took the eye and hearing tests, and went out to be tested on her bike. She did everything the examiner told her to do, very cleanly. The examiner, a short woman with braids wearing full leathers in the heat who didn't seem to actually sweat, graded her.

Corinne went in, and found out that she had completely passed all her tests. She combed her hair, used the lip gloss she remembered to stick in her jacket pocket. The DMV photographer took a picture that made it look like she was a felon for her brand-new motorcycle license. Mitch gave her a quick hug, and said, "Enjoy your new bike. I'm sorry, I don't have time to celebrate." He was gone before she had time to do anything other than give him a little wave goodbye.

*Time to celebrate,* Corinne thought. And she did, with her second can of Mountain Dew. She drove to Taco Bell on the way back to the holler, had some tacos with everything, and took two more of them back to the house with her.

Malcolm was up, and pacing. "Where have you been?" he asked.

"I told you about the exam last night. Had it so early in the morning that I seem to be a good thing to get it over with without waking you." Corinne stripped off her leathers, and put on shorts as fast as she could pull them on. There was a knock at the door. Corinne raised her finger. "That'll be the kid."

"What kid?" asked Malcolm.

"Not sure, Mitch found her." Corinne opened the door, and found a teenage girl with long, limpid brown hair and a plastic-braces smile standing on the other side of the door.

"I'm Lydia? Here to pick up the car? My dad will take us to get the title transfer signed?"

"Be down in a minute," said Corinne. She went over to the refrigerator, grabbed another Mountain Dew, grabbed a second one for the kid and a third for the dad, and said, "Malcolm, I've got to sign some stuff and turn in some paperwork. Relax, be back as soon as I can." She kissed him on the cheek as he stuffed his face with Taco Bell, then ran out the door and down the stairs.

Lydia's dad was a beanpole man with a shock of black hair on his head and a very manly beard, wearing jeans, a t-shirt, and work boots.

He was circling the car like a shark. Corinne introduced herself and gave him the keys, and he inspected the car from hood to hatch. Corinne gave one of the Mountain Dews to the kid, and she and Lydia talked about Lydia's high school classes while Lydia's father did his inspection. Lydia signed the green card and took the cash, then they all piled in to go to the DMV. That line actually went quickly, because Lydia's dad had his short, skinny son Jeb stand in line for him. Jeb got the last Mountain Dew that his father had rejected. They got everything squared away, then Jeb, Lydia's dad, Lydia, and Corinne all squished into the hatchback. They dropped Corinne off at home, and Corinne ran back upstairs, giving her red Harley a loving look on the way up.

By the time she got back upstairs, Malcolm was sitting on her cabbage rose chair, glaring at her. "Where the fuck did you go now?" he asked.

Corinne sighed,and grabbed another Mountain Dew. "I explained all this to you last night. I told you that I had a new bike, that I needed my motorcycle license before I could get my hands on it, that I was being tested this morning. I also explained that I was selling my old hatchback, and I was doing that this morning too. It's only half past eleven, and we have plenty of time to hike. Your Jeep will take us up the mountain much faster than my stupid car would anyway."

She finished off her Mountain Dew while she dressed for the hike. She had everything ready to go just inside her closet, a short-sleeved shirt, very thin but strong long hiking pants, heavy socks, and the light jacket to tie around her waist. Her hiking boots were at the door. She got the freezer packs out and filled up her jacket pockets. They would all melt their way into water soon enough. The picnic basket was ready to go, packed with whatever the hell Malcolm thought was a good idea to have for lunch. She double-checked her walking backpack, making sure there were plenty of snack bars and trail mix ready to go. She put on her backpack, grabbed her hiking shoes, and said, "Let's go, Malcolm!"

He groaned, grabbed the picnic basket, and followed her down the stairs. She put on her hiking boots while sitting on the bottom stair, then walked out to Malcolm's Jeep. He clicked it open with a beep, and she put her pack in the back and got into the front seat. Malcolm sighed, put the picnic basket in the back, and didn't bother checking any of his own equipment. He got in, shut the door, started the engine, made sure the air conditioning was on high. Malcolm turned the tunes up so loud she couldn't hear herself think. He screamed the lyrics to Tom Petty's "Running Down a Dream" as he drove off. Corinne was pissed that Malcolm was willing to annoy the neighbors, but he wasn't paying attention to Corinne to the point where berating him would work, anyway.

They followed the signs to the bottom of the trailhead, and they parked in the small lot. Corinne hopped out and took out the picnic basket and her own backpack. Mitch took out his much bigger pack, complete with bedroll and tent. "What do you need all that for?" asked Corinne. "You didn't say anything about spending the night. We're going to need a lot more water and food if that's what you plan on doing, and I have to work tomorrow. I've got two new clients, as well as the clients I have in exchange for my bike."

"Ha!" said Malcolm. "I knew you couldn't afford that bike on your own!"

Corinne put her hands on her hips and stared at him. "I did afford it on my own. I've been working on Mitch's websites in between working on my clients. I've been working like a dog. What the hell is wrong with you, Malcolm?"

Malcolm sighed. "I come all this way, and you don't have time for me?"

Corinne laughed. "I haven't heard from you in four months, and you show up completely unannounced with some plan in your head. I told you all my plans, and you didn't tell me any of yours. Except for the fact we were hiking, with no mention about spending the night. My suggestion is that you leave the tent, and I have a tarp for us to eat lunch." She grinned.

Malcolm snorted. Corinne sighed, and covered herself from head to foot in both insect repellent and sunblock. Malcolm did the same, and threw his tent and bedroll back in the truck with ill-mannered grace. Corinne smiled winningly at him, took out her water and took a sip, put it back, and started walking. He caught up, then Malcolm started walking a bit faster.

Corinne chatted, and because he obviously hadn't listened to anything she had said the night before, went over her life again since graduation. She talked about making dents on her school loans, building complicated websites that she never thought she'd take a crack at, and asked Malcolm questions about the apps he had been building at the company in Boston. Malcolm was his old self, determined not to talk about himself except through stories, asking Corinne more questions. He did talk about trips, especially Yosemite. He talked about wanting to move to Las Vegas, and maybe work for a gaming company there.

They came out on a wide vista, mountains hazy in the distance, green trees everywhere, and Corinne called a halt. She ate a trail mix bar and drank some water, and put her backpack down with relief. She slipped her phone out of her pocket, but found no bars. She put it back.

"We can have a picnic here," said Malcolm.

"We both just ate a few hours ago. I thought you wanted to do that by the pool, go swimming." Corinne laughed. "It's cooler up here, but not by that much. Hot enough to melt paint here around here most of the time."

Malcolm gave her a baleful glare. "Sure, honey."

"Great, sugar bear," said Corinne, in a sarcastic voice.

Malcolm sipped his own water, then walked around, first to the lookout point then back behind Corinne, then back to the point. Corinne stretched her legs, put her arms over her head and leaned back. She felt her back pop, and relaxed into it. She went over to the lookout point, and stood off to the side. She took out her cell phone, and started taking pictures. The lookout was gorgeous, showing the deep blue majesty of the mountains. She grinned, happier than she'd been in days.

Malcolm brought over her pack, knelt, and opened the flap. Corinne looked down at him, and smiled. 'I've got peanut butter bars, and I've got..." Her jaw hit the ground when Malcolm grabbed the backpack by one of its straps, took two steps forward, and threw it off the edge of the cliff. Corinne took a step forward, then shrugged. "I don't know what your major damage is, but that's just stuff. I can always replace it."

Corinne turned to walk away, and Malcolm knocked the phone out of her hand, then stomped on it with a resounding crack. Corinne knew something was seriously wrong when she saw the look of complete flatness in his eyes. She turned to run, but he grabbed her hand and swung toward her jawline. She ducked, but not fast enough. She twisted her head to the side, and felt the blow against her eye. It felt as if her whole entire eye would explode. She lifted her arm up and twisted it to the side, breaking his hold. She turned to run again, and leapt forward as he grabbed her arm. Her shoulder dislocated with a sickening crunch. She whirled, and without thinking, kicked him in the balls, punched him in the solar plexus, and hit him in the throat as hard as she could. She somehow got the hand from her bad arm into her pocket as she ran.

# ESCAPE

*C*orinne stayed away from the main trail, because she knew that's where Malcolm would look first. She found a goat trail and ran headlong down the narrow path. She was absolutely delighted that she had been stupid enough to forget to put on the orange vest she was supposed to be wearing to prevent someone from shooting her while walking in the woods. It would have been far too easy for Malcolm to track her if she had. The vest was in her backpack at the bottom of the lookout. She ducked around trees, jumped fallen logs, and weaved in and out of the little trail to be sure that he couldn't track her. She stood, gasping, and took a swallow of water from the bottle still in her other pocket. She went up to a tree, gauged the angle, and slammed her arm back into the socket against the tree. She screamed, trying to choke it back, afraid that Malcolm would find her. She let out another choking scream as she got her hand back into her pocket to keep the arm immobile.

She ran again, and wondered why she was having trouble seeing. She reached with her left hand and brushed the blood out of her rapidly closing left eye. She tried wiping the blood on her jeans, and was surprised to find that her fingers had trouble moving. Clocking him in the throat with a closed fist was probably not her brightest moment, but she had to keep moving. She found the goat trail again and tried to keep a steady clip. She remembered the last time she saw Jeopardy with her landlord. She started at the beginning, and replayed the entire show in her mind, whispering the answers to herself as she plunged down the trail.

Corinne slowed and then halted when she saw what looked like a dog with the pack on its back. It had a black nose and blue eyes, tufted ears with gray inside, and a brown coat with gray on its paws. She slowed, and kept thinking wolf, dog, wolf, dog. She figured it was a wolf-dog, a combination of the two. She held out the flat of her left hand, and wolf-dog sniffed her hand. It turned to the side, exposing the backpack. She unzipped the bright orange backpack, and was delighted to find a first-aid kit. She dropped the kit, groaned, then knelt onto the loamy ground. She pulled out some alcohol wipes and hissed as she cleaned the cut over her eye. She found a wide bandage and taped it over her eye, pressing down to be sure the blood didn't flood into her eye again.

Corinne looked down at her arm, tucked into the waistband of her jeans. Inside the kit she found a cylinder bandage, and a small scissors. She threw a length around her neck and held it with her teeth while she cut it with her left hand. The scissors were small, but worked well enough that she was able to cut off a long length. She tied the end together using her teeth and her good hand, and let out a yelp when she managed to get her recently-dislocated right arm into the other end. She wrapped another length around her shoulder, and tied it off under her arm. She checked out her hand, and used the rest of this cylinder to wrap up her swollen knuckles.

Corinne managed to zip the backpack again, and the wolf-dog looked her in the eyes. For some reason, she wasn't terrified. The dog turned, and trotted down the goat path, turning to make sure that she was following. "I'll take wolf-dogs for fifty, Alex," she said to the imaginary game show host in her head. She tried to lengthen her strides to keep up with the hybrid dog, making sure not to slip on rocks, leaves, or sticks. She had to step over branches and downed trees. She slipped into a military cadence song, something she'd heard on some movie long ago. She was having trouble remembering Jeopardy, and she realized she needed water. She stopped, sipped, and fished around for another bar. She couldn't find one, and gave up. She trotted off after the wolf-dog, moving as fast as she could without twisting an ankle.

The wolf-dog halted, and Corinne stumbled to a halt behind him. He walked to the edge of the trail, and looked back. She stared at him as if he'd said something terrible to her. "Where are you taking me?" she asked the wolf-dog. She looked down the embankment, and realized there was actually a section that looked like an old stream bed. It seemed to be free of everything but small sticks and leaves. She groaned, knowing that the dog wanted her to go down.

Corinne stretched out her back. Her body groaned as the recently dislocated shoulder made itself known. "Freaking dog, you better know exactly what you're doing." She sighed, sat in the stream bed, and started to slowly scoot her way to the bottom. She slid on the wet patch of leaves, and went down quite a ways on her butt. She managed to spread her feet out and catch herself, then went down more slowly, groaning with pain.

She managed to lean forward, step forward with her right leg, then right herself with the left. She stood there, attempted to brush off her jeans, and gave up. Swinging her hips around made her yelp with pain from the arm. Then, she stared when the wolf-dog sat and howled. It wasn't the *aroo* of *I'm here*, it was one of *danger here*. Corinne got over her initial startlement and said, "You better not have brought Malcolm down on us." She sighed, stood, and damn near fell over when there was an answering *aroo* from somewhere way down the mountain. She started following the wolf-dog again, surprised to find themselves on an actual path, widened and tamped down, with wooden beams when they had to step down or up. The hybrid dog sat down and *arooed* again, and there was an answering howl from down at the bottom of the mountain again. "Aren't wolf-dog supposed to be unable to howl?" she asked the canine. The wolf-dog gave her a wolfy grin and started trotting down the path.

Corinne heard noises and ducked down behind a tree log. A man with piercing dark eyes, very short black hair, and a strong jaw stepped forward, hands splayed out, and said, "I'm James. From what my brother said about the new woman in town, I think you met my brother Mitch. He sold you a bike." James was wearing a loose blue t-shirt, battered blue jeans, and hiking boots. He was clean-cut and looked a bit like an older, calmer, wiser Mitch, so Corinne felt herself relax a hair. She remembered his buying rope at the hardware store. The man stared at the wolf. "Go on now," James said to the hybrid. The wolf-dog raised its hackles and pretended to growl at James, but trotted off.

Corinne stared at the man. She could see echoes of Mitch in his face, but James had a wider face and darker eyes. "I'm Corinne. My friends-with-benefits Malcolm decided to flip out and throw my pack over the edge and smash my cell phone, then took swings at me." She eyed James warily as he looked at her head, her shoulder, and her other hand.

"Corinne, like I said, I'm James, and the last thing I would ever do is hurt you. But I do want to lift up your shirt a little bit on the side. From the way you're carrying yourself, I think you've got a cracked rib or two. I'd like to bind it up, and it will make a difference as to how to get you down this mountain."

Corinne didn't trust herself to speak. She just nodded, and then regretted it as her shoulder made itself felt. She gritted her teeth, and stood still while James pulled up first one side, then the other of her shirt. James touched her left side with the tip of one finger, and she reached up with her left hand and took a swing at him without realizing she was doing it.

James jumped back, hands up. "I'm really sorry. I think this proves that you have at least a cracked rib. I'm going to put down my backpack, and take out some more of that wrap in order to bind your ribs at the bottom. We don't want you suddenly being unable to breathe because your rib punctured a lung, do we?"

Corinne stood still again and said, "Is that a trick question?"

James snorted, dropped his bright blue backpack, and fished out another cylindrical rolling bandage. "No, it isn't." He took out a folding knife, and cut away the bottom of her shirt. He wrapped her up as gently as he could, and she hissed and tried not to hit him again. He tied off the end, and took some carabiners out of his backpack and three bungee cords.

"Here's where it gets really weird, Corinne," James said. "I can't carry you in my arms, because that you'll lean forward and you might get a punctured lung. You also have a damaged shoulder and hand, and you can't hold me around the neck. A fireman's carry would have the same problem. What I propose to do is to tie you to my legs, and walk down with you standing on my feet. You've got little feet, even in those hiking boots, and I can get you down much faster that way. We could send in a chopper, but by the time it got here, we could already be down the mountain."

Corinne nodded. She regretted that when her head swam, and said, "Do whatever you have to do to get me the hell out of here."

James set about attaching Corinne to his body. He put her feet on his, then tied her feet to his with bandage wrap. He used bungee cords to attach her legs to his, and was pleased to find that their knees met when she stood on his feet. He carefully wrapped bungee cords around her waist, and she screamed when he had to thread it under her damaged arm. "I am so sorry," he said. "I just don't want to damage your lungs."

"It's okay," she said. "I know that you have to do what you have to do."

"It doesn't mean I like hurting people," he said. "I know this is horrific for you."

Corinne gritted her teeth, and said, "Get me the complete and total hell down this mountain."

"On it." She clenched her teeth. James had his arms around her, holding her arm still, and her other arm was clamped around his arm that was around her waist. He kept up a steady pace, not daring to move too quickly, but he had his hiking stick. He used it to make sure that he wouldn't tip over with a woman attached to him.

"Faster," said Corinne, through clenched teeth.

"Absolutely," said James. He picked up the pace, and she hissed in a breath and held on tighter, her nails digging into his hand. He kept talking into his mic, and was horrified to find the EMTs were still forty minutes out, caught at an accident two mountains over. He increased the pace a bit more, making her hiss, but he knew he had to get her down. He listened carefully to her ragged, shallow breathing, concerned that she would puncture a lung.

James told Stretcher and Jared that he was on his way down, and for them to run up with a backboard. He heard pounding feet before he saw them. It wasn't a regular backboard, more a plank with holes punched into the wood, and one of those wraparound neck pillows used for airplane travel. James desperately hoped that would work. They came running up, but waited till he got to a flatter spot to make the transfer. Stretcher got on one side, her arms like ropes, and Jared the other, his dark skin glistening with sweat. They undid the bungee cords one by one, and slid the backboard down onto James' toes. They used the bungee cords to attach Corinne to the board Stretcher's muscles stood out as she picked up the head, and Jared had the feet. James jogged after them, delighted that the injured Corinne was very literally out of his hands.

At the bottom of the mountain where the ground evened out, Jared and Stretcher had backed up the big blue truck, the one they used to haul firewood around. Stretcher and Jared's father Gunny owned dozens of acres, and they sold small amounts of lumber, primarily deadfall and kindling. Forest fires were no joke. James hopped up and back, as they tied her to the bed with more bungee cords hooking onto the backboard. He knelt next to her head. "We're going to get you to the ambulance. Damn thing is still a few minutes out, so we need to get you there." James held her hand, and she clenched it.

James patted on the back window, and sat down on his ass, wedging her in place with his feet. Stretcher got on the other side and did the same thing. Jared, the driver, took it easy, darting over and around the potholes. Stretcher took her other hand and said, "Name's

Stretcher. Sorry it's so rough, but we're dodging potholes." Stretcher jabbed a finger at the tween girl crouched near Corinne's feet, and said, "This is Sylvie. She's going to do some things, and it's going to hurt like hell, but they never happened."

Sylvie stuck her face down toward Corinne's side. She had bright blue eyes, her blonde hair stuffed under a baseball cap. "This is going to hurt like a mother," she said in her piping tween voice. Stretcher clenched one hand and James the other. Sylvie stuck her hand below the wrappings on her side. She said things that didn't make any sense, and that was some crackling and popping that made Corinne cry out and hold onto James hand. There was an audible crunch, and Corinne went dead white.

"That's enough, Sylvie. She can't take much more, and you can't do it all." Sylvie's hands went out from under the bandage,and traveled up to Corinne's shoulder. The incomprehensible words came out again, and there was some sort of heat and crunching, and the pain made Corinne scream and turn sheet-white again. Then James said, "Stop." He hit the back window, and someone in a black helmet came up on a bike. They ground to a halt, and Stretcher handed Sylvie over the edge to the back of the bike. James hit the back of the truck window again, and the truck went forward. James looked down at Corinne, and said, "I know that hurt like glass under your skin. I'm really sorry. But, that never happened. Do you understand?"

Corinne side-eyed him. "What are you blathering on about? Injured woman trying to get to the hospital here."

Stretcher coughed out a laugh. "I like this one," she said to James. "What happened to you anyway? Did you think it's a good idea to slam into trees?"

"Malcolm did this," said Corinne. "Threw my backpack off the ridge, crushed my cell phone under his foot. He's never been violent before, friends with benefits, last name Kruger." She talked through clenched teeth. "Got him in the face, the balls, solar plexus. Can't be sure if he'll need or seek medical attention. He's a head taller than me, black hair, dark tan, bright green eyes, little scar on his right cheekbone, says he got a falling off a bike as a kid. Brought his Jeep and left my beautiful bike at home. Think the license plate has an X and a J in it, Arkansas plates, which is weird, because he said he got a job in Boston."

"Asswipe," said Stretcher. She pulled out her cell phone, and texted with one thumb while still holding onto the backboard.

They heard the siren long before they actually saw the ambulance. It slowed down, then made a K turn on the narrow road. The truck left them room to fling open the doors. Two came rushing out with the stretcher, and whistled at the improvised backboard. "Shit," said the woman on the right. "What the hell did you use, a door panel?"

"I call that improvisation with a purpose," responded James. "Probable broken ribs, dislocated right shoulder."

"Who the hell tuned you up?" asked the male EMT.

Stretcher held up her cell phone. "Sheriff has the info. Some guy named Malcolm, black hair, green eyes. If he comes in because she fought back, don't let him anywhere near her."

"Got it," said the woman EMT. "This is gonna hurt like a son of a mother but we've got to get you onto the stretcher and into our bus. You up for that?"

"I got a choice?" asked Corinne, through gritted teeth.

"Nope," said the male EMT. They left the improvised backboard the way it was, and Stretcher held her hand while James helped them get her out of the cab of the truck and onto the rolling stretcher. Corinne grunted out a laugh when she saw Stretcher and James play rock-paper-scissors for who rode with her. James won, paper over rock, and hopped in with her.

The male EMT drove all the female EMT stayed in back. She took vitals, while James spoke with Mitch on his cell phone, giving him the details. "I'm Antonia," said the female EMT. "Munoz apologizes for all the times he hits potholes."

Munoz snorted up front. "Doesn't matter how many times they grade this road, the potholes have relations with each other, and multiply. Kinda like dust bunnies."

Antonia grunted. "Classy, Munoz. We could technically go urgent care, be closer, but I think you need a real hospital to check you over. You got punched in the face, could have a head injury."

"Don't think so," said Corinne. "No double vision, vomiting, that sort of thing."

"Still, no use being stupid."

"Hate the stupid," agreed Corinne.

# HOSPITAL

*a* doctor and a nurse were ready at the doorway to the emergency room. The nurse snorted at the improvised backboard, and said, "We'll hold onto the bungee cords for you."

James snorted back. "What the hell did you think was going to happen? Mountain. Limited number of materials. Got her down alive, didn't we?"

The doctor waved her hand, brushing away all talk of bungee cords. Antonia reported blood pressure, blood oxygen levels, injuries, temperature, pointed out the i.v., and the dose of morphine. The doctor said, "Let's get her to x-ray. Broken ribs are nothing to mess with. I'm Dr. Hatch, Corinne. I'm very glad that you made it off the mountain so quickly. We are very happy we don't have to treat you for exposure."

Corinne still held James' hand. "Me, too. Let's get me patched up, and get me back home."

"Feisty," said the nurse.

"Stop mansplaining my patient to me, Mr. Diggs," said Dr. Hatch. She started rattling off instructions, as both Antonia and Corinne glared at Diggs. The nurse pushed Corinne down the hall to X-ray while the doctor went to make notes on her newest patient.

Sheriff Jude Hardest and Deputy Gomez came rushing up to James, Gomez keeping her gun from bouncing with her hand. "She's in x-ray," said James, shaking out his hand, after Corinne had alternately crushed and clawed it. "Don't know if the doctor or tech will let you in." Hardesty was a police chief, a weathered Cheyenne ex-Marine. He spoke to everyone with respect, but absolutely nobody messed with him. Gomez was young, but far from stupid. She had been a cop for two years, and was missing two fingers on her left hand because she'd also been in the military defusing bombs. They wouldn't let her back in the bomb squad after she'd lost the fingers, then two of her friends were killed. Annoyed and heartsick, she mustered out and moved back to the small town where she grew up. Hardesty hired her in a hot minute. She wore her black hair in a French braid, and always moved like she had a purpose.

Deputy Gomez gave Hardesty the side-eye, and he nodded, barely a tip of his chin. Gomez was off like a shot toward x-ray. "Where does this woman live?" Hardesty asked James.

"She's a tenant with Miz Raynelle Withers. Lives in that little place over the carport," said Mitch, coming up behind James. He was dressed in his full motorcycle clothes. Hardesty talked into his mike, gave the address to dispatch. "I sold her a bike, been teaching her to ride." Mitch handed over his phone. "While my brother was getting the woman down the mountain, I found Juniper Point where her asshole boyfriend threw her backpack over the side. I also found a smashed cell phone up there. I didn't touch either one of them, but I took pictures."

Hardesty scrolled through Mitch's pictures, handed back the phone, and said, "I'll go up there with Gomez as soon as she comes back out from interviewing the victim. I'm assuming you know exactly where to find these things?"

"Follow my bike," said Mitch. "And, blood, lots of boots scuffing, what I think are fibers on a tree on a goat path from where she popped her shoulder back in."

Hardesty winced. "Tough person," he said. Hardesty's phone pinged, and he saw Mitch had sent the pictures to his phone.

"What happened?" Hardesty asked James. James repeated what he had been told.

"What the hell was the perpetrator's major malfunction? " wondered James.

"Seems to me you throw someone's backpack over the edge of a lookout and smash the cell phone when you plan to do harm. And hide the victim's body." Hardesty's voice was ice cold.

"I'm assuming she met the guy in college. We talked about bikes, her work making websites. Never about ex-boyfriends." Mitch rattled off the name of the college, a small one hours away.

Hardesty looked up a number on the Internet, and made a call. He listened, said nothing, then looked up another number. He stepped away to chat with someone, obviously another law-enforcement person. He stepped back over to the brothers. "Unfortunately, gradua-tion happened, and the school's office is closed today. Someone has to go down there with a warrant to find things out. Got a call into local law enforcement."

"You see this one at your brother's house?" Hardesty asked James.

"Nope," said James. "There is this black and gray wolf-dog, very nice, we feed it sometimes." Mitch snorted. "Heard the thing howling up a storm, worried he ran into a bear or something. I went up there double-time, found the woman, but couldn't carry her down between her arm and the broken ribs. I called down for help. Had bungee cords in my pack, use them to tie the woman to me so we could get the hell down the mountain. Was terrified she was gonna puncture a lung along the whole damn way down. The people at the bottom ran up with a contraption so we could get her down without puncturing her lung. Put in the back of the truck, got her to the ambulance. Didn't know her from Adam, or Eve. Knew my brother had some woman he was trading a bike for cash and some websites named Corinne, but never met the woman before. Saw her once at the hardware store." And liked what he saw, but he shelved the wildly inappropriate thought.

Gomez came back, her stride long. "Spoke to the victim, Corinne Jackson. The attack didn't take long. Happened on Juniper Outlook.

He threw her backpack over, smashed her phone, ripped it right out of her hands. Laid hands on her, she fought back, got a shoulder dislocated for her trouble. X-ray tech says cracked ribs, her left eye is already swelling shut, no concussion despite the blow. Says she ducked a bit, or she'd be laid out for sure. She defended herself, got a few licks in. Ran off the main trail on some sort of animal track to get away from him. Popped her shoulder back in. Says she met some big wolf-dog who led her down some hillside to the main trail. Says James here met her, tied her to his body, and walked her down the mountain. Says some people in the truck drove her to the ambulance, got her here. Says she met the perp in college, had an on-again-off-again thing, says a man's like a breeze, blows in, they have fun, listen to some music, travel around, have a beer or two, then he breezes back out. I tried to call the college on my way back up. Got an out of office message."

"Already on it with local law enforcement," said Hardesty. He texted her the pictures that Mitch had texted him. "Call the techs. We're going to follow Mitch up the mountain, take our own pictures, take the evidence back down. These two gentlemen back up everything, including the big wolf-dog. Woman didn't hit her head, did she?"

"The woman didn't have any symptoms," said Gomez. "In pain but clear as a bell. She's some sort of web designer. Says she's been working for Rachael and Mitch here, plus some online clients."

"As far as I know, she never met Rachael, even today," said Mitch. "They have been doing all their business by email and phone."

"I think I know the goat trail she took," said Gomez. "Said she had to ride on her ass down to the main trail, said the dog wouldn't move until she did. If she had gone any farther, she would've fallen off a damn cliff. Goats could've gone down, but a human woman couldn't have. That dog saved her life."

James carefully didn't look at Mitch. "We'll be happy to take her home, or wherever the heck she wants to go, if they let her out today."

"Can't believe some monster decided to beat the hell out of a woman for no particular reason. We'll keep an eye out for her until you catch this guy," said Mitch.

"You know her well?" asked Gomez.

"Even on the ass-end of nowhere, I have better Internet than she does where she lives. It was in my best interest to let her work at my place sometimes when I was out pounding on the bikes. She's been over five, maybe six times in the past few weeks. Had lunch a couple times, some sandwiches and chips, and I kept the refrigerator full of sodas. Woman loves her caffeine." Mitch grinned. "Brother dearest was never there at the time. She also likes barbecue and bought some from me."

James nodded. "Would have remembered her if I had. Even all banged up, she's one hell of a beautiful woman."

Gomez and Hardesty put away their little notebooks. "You call me if you remember anything else, or talk to Gomez," said Hardesty. "And if you do run across the guy, it's okay if he falls down a few times, but I need him in good enough condition to prosecute the hell out of him. Call me immediately, and be damn careful, because bullies are usually weaklings. Son of a gun might be armed."

Mitch's eyes flashed, and James' eyes went flat. "He better not come back when I can see him," said Mitch, his voice a low growl. "She's a real nice woman, certainly didn't deserve some piece of trash knocking her around like that."

James nodded at the sheriff. "I'll hogtie him and call you if I see him"

"Be damn careful," reiterated the sheriff. "And we will look real deep at his past. Guys like this usually don't turn it on and off like a switch. My guess is he's done something to someone else, possibly something very bad."

Mitch's eyes narrowed, and James nodded once. "Will make sure nothing happens to her while you conduct your investigation," said James. "And I would find out where this malicious monster has hiked before."

"On it," said Hardesty. His phone buzzed, and he looked at it. "My deputy already knows where the spot is, but I'll follow you, Mitch.

Don't want to get lost on the damn mountain. We will follow the trail, mark her passage down to where she met James. Get plenty of evidence to shut the door on this guy."

"Say hi to Tuck the Tech for me," James said to his brother.

"Will do," said Mitch. Hardesty and Gomez followed him out to his bike.

James found the doctor. "I know you can't tell me about her condition. But she's my brother's friend, I want to see if she's getting admitted, or if she needs a ride somewhere."

Dr. Hatch nodded. "She doesn't show any signs of a concussion and has no head or neck injuries. The perpetrator who hit her didn't break any bones in her face, and she seems to have had some brains when she fought back and mostly used the flat of her hand. So, she didn't break any knuckles. You already knew about the other injuries, so I don't think that's a doctor-patient confidentiality violation. She's in exam three, I'll walk you there."

They went down the hall to the emergency room. Corinne had her arm in a sling, and an i.v. in the other hand. The wound over her eye was stitched and bandaged. She was as pale as her pillow. Corinne looked up. "Dr. Hatch, James. To what do I owe the pleasure?"

"As I told you a few minutes before, you can be released, if you have someone to care for you. It is absolutely no fun to do everything one-handed with broken ribs," said the doctor.

James stepped forward. "Mitch is going up to the site, up on the mountain because he found where the attack happened and he took the sheriff up there. I know it's weird that we haven't met, but I'm Mitch's brother. Anyway, I do really live there, but I'm gone a lot. As you know, there are three bedrooms. We also, apparently, have better Internet than your place. I know Miz Raynelle's place is over a garage. Stairs are gonna hurt like hell. I know we're guys, but we know some females who can help us. Would you like to live with Mitch and I for a few weeks while you recover?" Her eyes got cloudy. The fear in them made him quail and rage at the same time. He carefully made his voice soft. "I'll be out on trails. I've got fishing, hiking booked. I'm a guide.

Mitch will be there pounding away on bikes in his garage. You can just rest."

Corinne snorted. "A few weeks? I hope it's more like a few days. If Mitch says it's okay, sure, that sounds good. He makes a real good pulled pork sandwich." She accidentally moved and groaned. "Doc, a little more pain meds? If I'm traveling, that means I need to get into somebody's truck. I sure as hell am not going on the back of a Harley."

Stretcher popped her head in. "There you are. How's the patient?"

Corinne narrowed her eyes. "Banged the hell up. Dr. Hatcher was about to get me some more meds before throwing me out to the cold, cruel world."

Dr. Hatch grinned. "Let's get you a shot in that i.v. before we take it out." She looked over at James. "No stairs?"

"Absolutely none," said James. "There is a bedroom and bath on the ground floor."

"We brought a truck," said Stretcher. "It's in the lot." The doctor nodded and left.

James nodded. "You wanted pulled pork. Got any other things you really want? We can pick some stuff up on the way back."

"Right now, my stomach is too churned up to think about that. But, I love mint cookie ice cream, Oreos, and both apple and pecan pie." When they both stared at her, she said, "What? Oh, and Cool Ranch Doritos." She tried to shrug, and groaned. "One, I work with computers and love caffeine and sugar, and two, I eat sugar when I get upset. Right now, I'm upset."

"You should be," said James.

"I would be, too," said Stretcher.

"Actually, if I saw Malcolm again, I'd remove his face." Corinne flexed her good hand.

"We'll help you do it," said James. The nurse came back with a shot, then removed the i.v.. Stretcher handed Corinne the t-shirt she had tied around her waist. "Nice and clean, from my gym clothes bag." Stretcher turned. "Out," she said to James. There was some screaming as they got the shirt and the sling on Corinne, then Stretcher took Corinne's good arm and helped her into the wheelchair. Stretcher pushed her out to the front door while Corinne sat there with a chalk-white face.

James stood with her in the sunshine while Stretcher went to go get the truck. Jared, the driver, had called a friend to pick him up. "Sheriff Hardesty and Deputy Gomez are working hard. They'll find Malcolm."

Corinne nodded once, squinting against the light. "I need to swing by my place, pick up some stuff." Stretcher pulled up. "Let's do this thing," she said.

# FLOW

They kicked James out at the store. Stretcher took Corinne by her apartment, and helped her hiss and cuss her way up the stairs. Corinne pulled out the duffel bag one-handed, and Stretcher put whatever Corinne pointed out into the bag. Corinne kept up a steady stream of cursing, as she went through her house trying to figure out which she needed to take with her. She was very pissed off at having to pack up her laptop one-handed, but pulled it off by turning the air blue. Stretcher tried to help, but backed off when faced with Corinne's angry glares. Stretcher did manage to carry the stuff down and put it in the vehicle, then go back up and walk Corinne back down super-slowly.

Her landlord came by, listened to James explain the situation, and was very happy that Corinne was getting taken care of somewhere else. Stretcher explained what happened, "Woman like me got no call taking care of some girl who can't move her arm. Man do something like that, he be lower than a snake's belly. What are people doing to find that snake in the Garden of Eden?"

Stretcher said, "Ma'am, the sheriff's gonna look for this guy real hard. He's got tanned skin, black hair, and green eyes. You see anybody come around you don't like, you call the sheriff's office. You tell the neighborhood people to be watching too. He knows where she lives, but if he has any brains, he's running like a rabbit somewhere else."

Raynelle snorted. "Man like that, go hit on a woman in this day and age with cameras all around, he ain't got the brains God gave a snail. He might come round here, but we're country people. Boy's liable to get buckshot in his ass."

Corinne found a picture of Malcolm on online picture files using Stretcher's phone, sent it to the sheriff, and showed the file to her landlady. "You see this man, go right on ahead and shoot him in the butt."

Stretcher snorted as Corinne's landlady nodded. "Ain't no problem making that one regret his decisions."

"I hope that he does, ma'am," said Corinne. "He probably won't, though, not 'till he's been in jail for a couple of years. Then I bet my laptop that he'll blame it on everybody else except himself."

"Let's get you into the truck," said Stretcher.

"You go on now, ladies," said the landlady. "Ain't no call standing on this heat, you with the messed-up arm. You take care of yourself, hear? You can cut the rent down a little bit. 'Cause you won't be here using no electricity or nothin'."

Corinne turned to her landlady, shocked, and winced at the sudden movement. "Ma'am, don't you worry none. I can pay my debts, and I'm making good money now. Not the greatest, I'm not gonna get rich soon, but I've got enough. Don't you worry about the rent. You'll get it."

Raynelle subsided. Pride was something she understood. "How you goin' to do all that work with only one working arm?"

Corinne grinned. "One, I have websites that I change for each client. I'm not doing things from scratch. Two, I've got a speaking program that does everything but get your coffee. I had to use it when I broke my wrist when Tania, Kandace, and I decided to play tennis drunk." She smiled lopsidedly, despite the throbbing in her arm, face, and chest. "Stupid, but we sure as hell had a lot of fun back then."

Stretcher finished filling up the truck, and helped Corinne get in.

"We'll keep in touch, ma'am. You know our family. We will take very good care of her."

"I sure do know that," said the landlady. "Y'all go on now. Get better soon! I'll have my church pray for you."

"Thank you, ma'am," said Corinne, through the open window. "See you as soon as I can!"

They swung back and picked up James. Despite how tiny the grocery store was, he had three reusable bags full of food. Stretcher swung by the pharmacy while Corinne fished her wallet out of her bag of things the hospital had bagged of hers. She gave the bank card to James. Pharmacy bag in hand, James asked Stretcher to swing by Hardee's to get some chocolate shakes. Then, Stretcher took it slow to Mitch and James' A-frame house. Corinne drank her shake and swallowed her pills.

Back at James and Mitch's A-frame home, James walked Corinne to her room while Stretcher put the groceries away. Corinne found herself in a small room with a standard-sized bed, green plaid sheets, a tiny chest of drawers, and a plastic low bookshelf which she dragged over, one-handed, to her bed. She took over a week's worth of clothes, figuring they could either be washed or she could go back and get more.

James got Corinne cleaned up, moved the end of the couch with the recliner closer to the bathroom, covered that end with a sheet, and helped her sit with a pillow on her lap for her arm. James set Corinne up with a tray table laden with water in a blue and lemon lime soda in a purple sealed cup with integrated straw, some crackers, and her cell phone charger. He put a big bowl next to it in case she felt sick. James used her phone to set a timer so she knew when she could take the next dose, gave her the TV remote, and said, "Enough movement for one day. I suggest that you sleep."

"Like that's so easy," Corinne said. She had no idea how she could fall asleep while being in so much pain and filled with waves of sheer bloody-minded rage.

"Try," James said and, to her frustration, turned and walked away.

~

*J*ames brought her grilled cheese, tomato soup, and medicine when she woke up from her nap. Then, Stretcher came back to help Corinne shower. Stretcher helped Corinne undress, and got her into the shower one baby step at a time. Stretcher stripped down to her camisole bra and panties, both in a sky blue that contrasted with her dark skin. Stretcher had a long, thin, beanpole body with ropy muscles and small breasts. "Stop looking, I know you're not a lesbian," said Stretcher. "I am, and you don't float my boat." Corinne barked out laughter, holding her side in the sudden pain from her ribs, and Stretcher washed her back and hair and the side her good arm couldn't reach.

"Thank you," said Corinne, after Stretcher had dried Corinne off, helped her apply lotion, blow-dried her long hair, put in a quick braid, and helped her put on underwear and a camisole.

Stretcher laughed, dried herself off, and dressed again. She shrugged. "I hate unclean people. You smelled like you'd been rolling in dead leaves and blood. You offended me."

Corinne snorted. "I think I offended myself."

"James should have called me sooner," said Stretcher. "Girl stuff is not his forte."

Corinne made a face. "James and Mitch seem to be manly men. The downstairs bedroom is done in Early Male." Stretcher laughed as she rebound Corinne's ribs, got her in a loose shirt, got the sling on with a lot of screaming curses, rewrapped the damaged knuckles on her other hand, got shorts on her, and got her back to the recliner. Stretcher went to the kitchen and brought back ice packs for the shoulder, ribs, and hand. "My name is Corinne, and I'm addicted to ice packs," Corinne said, as she wiggled them around to get them in the right place.

Stretcher laughed, got the remote, plopped down in the other recliner, and put on a show about a woman who could walk through walls because of an ancient Egyptian amulet. They both made snide comments about the fight scenes and ridiculous dialogue. After the movie, James replaced the blue freezer packs and fed Corinne chicken noodle soup.

~

Corinne felt the screams rise in her throat. She wanted to thrash around, but something was on her lap. She reached out with her shaking good hand and felt fur. Her eyes flew open. She let the screams out and cried, tears dripping onto the fur. Blue eyes looked up at her. The wolf-dog licked her face.

James came thudding down the stairs, wearing shorts and nothing else. "Corinne! Oh, a nightmare." He took cautious steps forward. "I'm sorry. I'm a guy. Um, I'll get...a wet washcloth." He padded to the bathroom, came out, handed her the wet cloth.

Corinne kept kind of scream-crying and shuddering, which made her ribs hurt, so she moaned too. She heard James on the phone. Soon Stretcher was there. "Hey," Stretcher said. "Let it out. Go ahead."

"Hurts. Crying. Hurts. But. Can't. Stop."

"I hate to tell you, but you've gotta let it out. All the way out. Else those dreams will haunt you the rest of your damn life. I should know." Stretcher rubbed Corinne's good shoulder while the canine licked her tears away. She looked up at James. "James, I get that you're feeling helpless. I've got this. Get another wet washcloth and more pain meds. The patch on her shoulder won't keep up with this. Then, go to bed. You've got a fishing group in the morning."

James spread his hands. "I never regretted being a guy before."

Stretcher sighed. "If more guys felt that way, the less this kind of shit would happen. Go on, get her stuff." James sighed, and slunk off.

"Sorry. Not. Trying. To. Hate. On. Guys." Corinne tried to breathe, but breathing hurt. She took more shallow breaths. "Just. One. Guy. Didn't see. It coming."

"None of this was your fault." Stretcher's voice was clear. "Not one second. You thought you were hiking. He thought he needed to assault someone."

"How. Did. His. Mind. Go. There?"

"No clue. Not even from the dollar clue store. Not one."

James put the pills in Stretcher's hand, and Stretcher fed them to Corinne. James handed over the drinking cup with the straw in its lid. Corinne sipped lime water, choked. Sipped again. "I may have wanted to punch my brother in the nose." The wolf-dog whined. "It's a brother thing. I wanted to beat up some people from time to time. But, I got the hell over it. A man is in control of his emotions, or he needs to see a doctor to work it out. No urge to hurt a female, ever. Not even Cathy Quallen."

"She was a piece of work. Still is, I hear. Woman lies with nearly every breath."

"Know. Someone. Like. That." Corinne cleaned up her face. "Gonna lean back. Not move."

"Okay. I'll stretch out. Got a recliner on this end, too. Guard your sleep."

Corinne looked down at the wolf-dog. Her brain started to move its gears. "How did. Wolf-dog get in?"

Stretcher shrugged. "Back door didn't close all the way. I'll get myself a blanket. James, go the hell to bed. I've got this."

Corinne closed her eyes. "Good dog."

Stretcher laughed, and James retreated up the stairs. Corinne relaxed, finally, and sleep took her under.

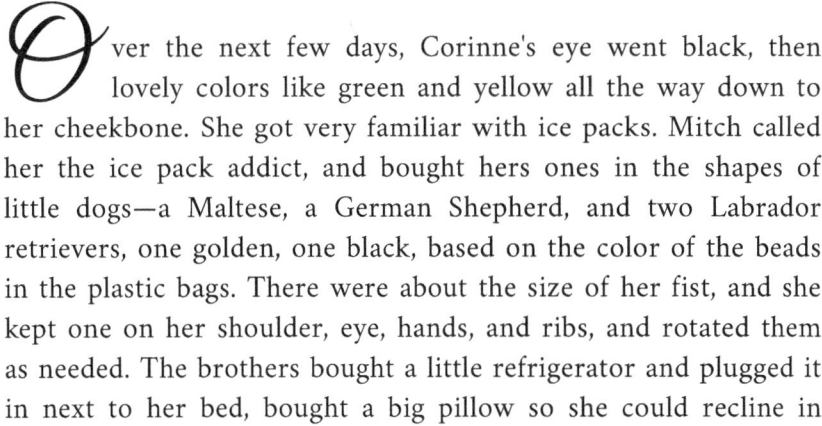

Over the next few days, Corinne's eye went black, then lovely colors like green and yellow all the way down to her cheekbone. She got very familiar with ice packs. Mitch called her the ice pack addict, and bought hers ones in the shapes of little dogs—a Maltese, a German Shepherd, and two Labrador retrievers, one golden, one black, based on the color of the beads in the plastic bags. There were about the size of her fist, and she kept one on her shoulder, eye, hands, and ribs, and rotated them as needed. The brothers bought a little refrigerator and plugged it in next to her bed, bought a big pillow so she could recline in bed, and they packed the tiny freezer portion full of the little ice packs.

She woke up screaming more than once. The wolf-dog would lay on her lap, and Stretcher would show up a few minutes later. James was sometimes gone. Mitch was apparently a heavy sleeper and slept through the screaming; he never came down to comfort her. Corinne felt so bad that she made James feel negatively about being a guy. Stretcher told her to get over her sympathy, that James knew one guy was not all guys. Corinne got it out; she was not going to wake up shaking, screaming, and crying forever. She felt her feelings, ranted against Malcolm. Finally, the dreams started to get farther and farther apart.

~

*J*t took nearly a week of sleep and streaming movies until Corinne was able to lose the nausea and focus enough to turn on her laptop. Corinne had Mitch plug in one of the screens and put it on a tray table so Kandace could lay back in the black recliner as she dictated what she wanted done on the websites with her wireless headphones. She got up only to grab a new soda, or switch over ice packs.

Corinne found that she could only work for about half an hour at a time before the pain really pissed her off. The whole point of work was to focus on something other than the sharp, shooting pain in her ribs, the vibrant all-over pain of her shoulder and eye, and the rapidly lessening pain in her hand. She would work, take a break, then dictate some more code, test it, fix the bugs, and do everything all over again. It was time-consuming, but after a while, like before, she was able to actually speak more quickly then she could type.

"Food time." James took the stairs down, two at a time.

"Don't you have someplace to be? Some trail to hike?"

James shook his head. "Call 'em lieu days. People don't hike on Monday, generally speaking, unless they're on vacation. I am usually gone from Thursday morning to Sunday night." He headed to the kitchen, made some noises, and came over to the couch with a plate of food, a small bag of chips, and a bottle of something with bubbles.

Corinne bit into a rotisserie chicken wrap with stone ground mustard, smoked bacon, and strips of carrots and red bell pepper. "Mmm," she said. She put down the wrap and added another line of code. "Ugh. This is so slow."

"If you stop coding, I'll open the Fritos for you."

"You are so cruel," Corinne said. "Hand me a Mountain Dew." She took her good hand off her keyboard.

"Nice try," James said. "Your doctors said no caffeine. I have strawberry-grape water."

"Mean." Corinne made a face. James poured fruit water into her cup and screwed the top back on. He opened the Fritos and added it to her plate, along with a tablespoon of dill-sour cream dip.

"Get much done today?" he asked, stealing a chip.

Corinne narrowed her eyes at him. "You are evil incarnate. I can only type or dictate for a while until the pain makes me homicidal."

"Sorry, one more hour on the pain meds," James informed her.

Corinne pointed a Frito at him. "Dictating is worse. The code has more bugs that way. And, this is a monster. Seventeen pages."

James grinned at her. "One minute at a time." Corinne gave him a one-finger salute with her bad hand that made her wince. James snorted and walked away.

～

The brothers were there every two hours with chips, sandwiches, wraps, flavored waters, and fruit juices since the doctor had her off the caffeine. Every four hours she got more meds; by Hour Three Corinne was actively snarling. To make everything worse, being without her Mountain Dew and Coca-Cola made her snarl, which just made Mitch and James laugh. Once she was able to get to the kitchen without throwing up, she found the motherlode in the freezer: Frozen pizza, Popsicles, and Ben & Jerry's ice cream. She told herself that she was going to be the size of a house, but the siren call of sugar was far too difficult for her to resist in her rage-y, painful state.

~

*R*ipley screamed at the alien queen during the *Alien* movie marathon. Mitch had his shirt off and black jeans on; he smelled like motor oil and hot metal. He got on his hands and knees and taped down the power cord with silvery duct tape. "You can see that from the moon," Corinne said, and stopped the movie. "What are you connecting to that monster power cord?"

James brought in a bright red box. "Special refrigerator-freezer," he said. "This is for your juice, ice packs, and ice cream so you won't have to go to the kitchen. Would have done this earlier, but Mitch was late."

"Working on a 2018 white Harley softail Fat Boy." Mitch tore the tape with his teeth. "Owner sold it due to cash flow after an accident. It's a beauty."

"White? Really?" Corinne said.

"Our girl likes red," Mitch said. "Hence the Coke fridge."

"And I can't have caffeine!" Corinne was stunned when she burst into tears.

"What the..." James said. He looked around, grabbed a box of tissues, took two out, knelt, and put them in Corinne's fingers.

Mitch laughed. "Your face, bro," he said.

"Try dealing with her claws all day," James said. He stood as Corinne dabbed at her eyes. "I know how to deal with this." He went to the galley-style kitchen across the back wall. He took a rounded carton out of the refrigerator, then grabbed a napkin and a spoon. "Halfsies special, chocolate mint cookie and peanut butter cup." He popped off the top, and handed her the spoon. He held out the pint. She took it, clenched it between her knees, and dug out the ice cream with her good arm. She put the spoon upside-down on her tongue and sucked.

"Wow. Instant lack of tears." Mitch plugged in the refrigerator and stood. "I'll get it cleaned out and fill it up later."

"I want the juice pops and the ice cream in there," Corinne said, pointing to her new little refrigerator. "And that yummy rotisserie chicken grape pecan chicken salad and crackers."

"Have to wait until the fridge gets cold," James said. He put the top for the pint on Corinne's little side table, and she dug in more.

"Tank oo," Corinne said, around more ice cream. Mitch came out, cleaned out the refrigerator, and transferred over the chicken salad and crackers. Then he made caramel popcorn and watched Ripley kick the alien queen's behind. He kept up snarky commentary that made his brother grunt and Corinne hit him with a pillow.

~

James took long trips, as summer was in full swing. People came from all around for him to act as their guide for rock climbing, spelunking, hiking, birdwatching, whitewater rafting, canoeing, kayaking, and fishing. The rivers were wide and meandering until they met, then they plunged down into a valley, creating some spectacular falls. James excelled at taking kids out in huge groups, fishing, hiking, or canoeing. He knew every scoutmaster and den mother in that segment of the state, and was often gone every single weekend, usually for three or four days at a time. Twice, he was gone for nearly a week.

James called random days during the week and one weekend a month his "lieu days," and spent those days sleeping, reading on the porch hammock, and eating like a horse. His muscles were taut. He was rangy, his tan merging with the brown of his hair, his eyes startling in his increasingly weathered face. He liked to sit out on the porch and whittle little owls, bears, horses, sheep, goats, wolves, badgers, and squirrels. He sold them online, and laughed when Corinne asked how much money he made from that. "Enough to pay my bills," he said. "My half of the power, water, and trash and recycling pickup bills, my cell phone, that sort of thing. Works nicely being a guide. My clients usually end up buying from me, too."

Mitch worked on his bikes all day, every day, unless his brother was home. Then, he usually took a day or two off. Corinne could hear what was playing in the workshop from time to time when things got particularly loud. Since she had headphones, she usually played her rock music loud enough to drown out his country rock, but from time to time she found herself singing along to "Sweet Home Alabama" or "Man, I Feel Like a Woman." The last song made her laugh until she stopped herself. Cracked ribs made laughter feel like she was being stabbed to death. Mitch had a newbie bike owner. He trained the young man in black leathers; they zipped up and down the drive. A few days later, the white Fat Boy was gone. "I tack on the price of my lessons to the cost of the bike," Mitch said when Corinne asked about it.

Corinne made a face at him, and looked out at the two parked Harleys Mitch had finished, a black Night Rod with its distinctive low-rise handlebar, and a 2018 Road King in Twisted Cherry. "Hey, you made me pay more!"

Mitch snorted. "Passed the driving tests, didn't you?"

"I did," Corinne said, grudgingly.

"Girl, when your three weeks of pain and anti-inflammatory pills are up, I'll personally pour a Mountain Dew down your throat."

"You better."

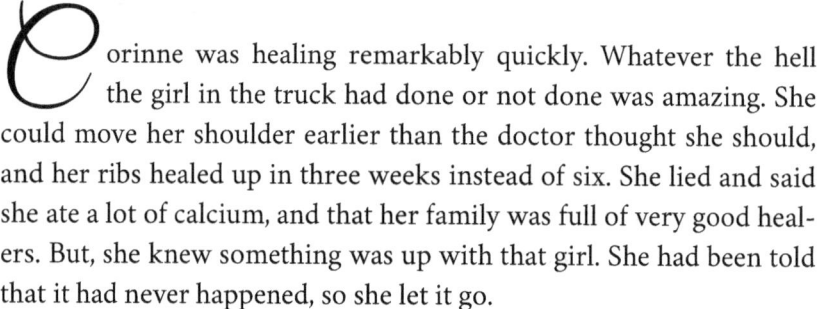

Corinne was healing remarkably quickly. Whatever the hell the girl in the truck had done or not done was amazing. She could move her shoulder earlier than the doctor thought she should, and her ribs healed up in three weeks instead of six. She lied and said she ate a lot of calcium, and that her family was full of very good healers. But, she knew something was up with that girl. She had been told that it had never happened, so she let it go.

Something was up with the brothers. No matter how nasty she

got, they let her growl, whine, curse, even throw pencils across the room. Mitch and James made a point of catching the pencils, and their ability to catch them absolutely amazed her. They could effortlessly snatch pencils out of the air. She dropped her butter knife once and Mitch had it back in her hand before she even registered that it had fallen. They had a foam basketball and net, and Mitch and James would both make shots from the other side of the huge room and get nothing but net.

They were also very sensitive about smell. Corinne learned never to eat tuna and found that the smell of bacon or pulled pork would get Mitch running in from outside, sweaty, with grease under his finger-nails from working on bikes. Then he would wash with Lava soap for five minutes at the sink before devouring the food.

Mitch made good money from selling bikes. He had clients come by all the time to try, then buy very expensive Harleys with bank transfers, even cash. He had his own credit card reader, too. He would sell the bike, go make a deposit in the bank if he needed to, pick up groceries, and cook steak, chicken, or pork on the back grill, along with red bell peppers, corn, and potatoes. Stretcher came in three times a week to give Corinne her bath. Corinne figured she was offending them all with her smell.

Corinne tried to figure out why James had been on that mountain on that particular day. He was always walking the mountain trails, but it was weird he'd been walking them without tourists. James said that he had been visiting the farm of a friend, and he heard the dog howl-ing. Corinne asked the name of the dog, and Mitch's face froze, while James doubled over laughing. "You see that dog again, call it Blackie. It's as good a name as any." Mitch slapped him on the shoulder, and then both men started laughing. Corinne had no idea what was so funny and decided that men were stupid.

*I*t was her third week, and Corinne was ready to kill everyone. There were only so many television shows and movies she could watch at night, exhausted from the pain. "Got an invitation to Rachael's farm," said James. Mitch's face got very still. "Since you ended up kind about their back door, they want to be sure that you're okay, Corinne." He smiled. "Plus, you built the farm a website."

"Why wouldn't I be okay?" asked Corinne. "I'm in pain, I walk like a geriatric, my work is going painfully slowly, I can't sleep at night, I want to sleep during the day, and I'm in so much pain in my brain from having no caffeine that I want to kill everyone. How do they feel about serial killers?"

Mitch snorted with laughter. "Sounds like Rachael on a good day. She's as ornery as you, but she makes the best steak and cornbread you ever had in your damn life."

"Cornbread," said Corinne, wistfully. "That sounds wonderful."

"And apple pie with cinnamon ice cream," said James, patting his stomach.

"You had me at food," said Corinne. "When do we go?"

# BARBECUE

Stretcher was at the diner, working her way through a plate of ribs. Stretcher stood, picked up a plate, and moved over to a bigger table. "Looks like the patient is up and around," she said, with a big smile.

"She's not patient at all," said Mitch. Corinne glared at him, and Stretcher snorted. He attempted to pull out a chair for Corinne, but she turned and went over to a long booth. She slid in and exhaled, exhausted after the walk into the diner in the heat.

"Looks like I'm moving," said Stretcher. She took her plate and silverware. Mitch followed with her glass of Coke, and James followed with her biscuits and butter on small plates.

Mitch slid into the booth next to Stretcher, and James slid next to Corinne. "That looks awesome," said James. He pointed down at the ribs and then at himself, and then held up an index finger. Mitch held up two fingers, and said, "I will slice up your ribs if you want some," he said.

Corinne held up three fingers, and said defiantly, "I want a damn Coke, and if any of you say anything I'm stabbing you with both my fork and my steak knife. And I'll do it one right after the other, so you won't have time to recover."

Stretcher looked from Corinne to a grinning Mitch, listened to James' chuckle. "So she's as bad as either one of you when she's hurt?" she asked. She shrugged at Corinne's flat stare. "What? I only see you a few times a week for about an hour."

Mitch nodded once, and said, "Corinne is like when James broke his foot and separated the tendon. But, I think she's a little less evil than me from when I broke both arms."

"How the fu...hell did you do that?" said Corinne, remembering at the last second she was in public and couldn't curse like a sailor.

James nodded to Sissy, the swing shift waitress and half owner of the barbecue joint who came over with the Cokes. "Thank you, darlin'," he said, with a grin. Sissy was almost sixty years old, gray hair braided down the back of her neck, but she blushed prettily anyway. "Hiking," he said, tersely. "My brother here went face first off the mountain. He forgot to tell you about the two black eyes, chipped teeth, and the bad attitude." He grinned. "I think it cost more to fix the teeth than did for anything else. He broke both arms because he was trying to stop his fall with his arms rather than drop and roll like I taught him."

"Jerk," said Mitch. "This fu...freaking idiot only got a few bruises. We decided to have it out over Mary Roane. I was fifteen, and he was sixteen. She was fifteen and a half. After that, she wouldn't give either one of us the time of day. She called us ruffians."

James laughed. "He had to look up the word, and then he was really polite and considerate for about two months." Sissy came out with the biscuits, and James split and buttered them for Corinne. The platters came out with the ribs, corn, and coleslaw. James took Corinne's corn, and cut it off the cob. Mitch sliced Corinne's pork ribs.

Sissy came out with a little bowl for the corn, and apologized. "Corinne, everyone knows damn well the reason why you haven't been back here is because you dislocated your shoulder. You're even wearing a bright blue sling. My stupid mind couldn't even figure out what needed to be done. I'm sorry about that."

Corinne shook her head. "I keep trying to reach with the wrong hand for stuff, and then wail when I realize that I'm being stupid. If

I'm the one with the injury and I forget about it, how should I expect everyone else to remember?"

"It's the heat," said Stretcher. "Melts everyone's brains. I went all the way to fix the fence and I forgot my damn wire cutters. Had to haul all the way back."

"Can't have those goats getting out," agreed Sissy.

"Goats? Not cows?" asked Corinne. "I thought everyone around here had dairy farms."

"Nope." Stretcher buttered her biscuit. "The operation may be loud and smelly, because the boys are smelly as hell, and the kids squeal a lot waiting for us to finish milking so they can get milk from their dams. We've got goat milk and kudzu eaters. Rachael makes and sells goat cheese. We take Bob and Henry all over the state. We have a special contract for Bud and Lou. They are on the side of the highway somewhere on any given weekday. Got little orange vests for them and everything."

Corinne laughed. "I've got to see the goats in vests sometime." She sucked in a breath when she accidentally moved her shoulder.

Everyone was quiet while they lit into the food. Sissy, the server with strong arms from smoking racks of ribs and a huge Southern smile, came out with the carafe of Coke so she didn't have to keep filling up the glasses. They ate like wolves, and didn't stop until there was absolutely nothing on any of the plates.

Sissy came out and cleared the plates. "Y'all have room for dessert?"

"Apple pie with cinnamon ice cream," said Corinne. "Been thinking about it all day."

The rest of them all held up forefingers, and Sissy laughed. "That's why this barbecue house has been winning awards for going on forty years. My mama is eighty-two years old, and still makes those pies every damn day. Says it's the best part of her day, too. Best pie in three counties. Be right back." She turned to go put in the order.

"So what's it been like living with these two ruffians?" asked Stretcher.

Corinne laughed. "I don't see either one of them that much, except for eating time." She shook her head. "That really isn't true. Mitch is in every two hours to be sure I have me some snacks, hands me a new drink. He also laughs at me when I try to make sandwiches one-handed."

James narrowed his eyes at his brother. "What? It's funny!" Mitch defended himself.

Now Corinne narrowed her eyes at him. "Not so funny when you have to clean the floor because I dropped the mustard or the knife."

Mitch hung his head. "Sorry, Corinne," he said. "Ruffian, remember?" He flexed his biceps, and made Corinne laugh. He was always doing stretches, lunges, burpees, push-ups. He said it made the blood flow to his fingers so that he could work on bikes more easily.

James groaned. "Stop showing off, little brother."

"Hear you been logging a lot of hours in the SUV," said Stretcher, quietly, to James.

"Have," he said, equally quietly. "I still do the overnights on weekends, but breakfast needs cooking on weekdays." He smiled affectionately. "Little bro likes to sleep in, does nothing but scratch and groan like a caveman until he's put at least one part on a bike."

Mitch lowered his head, looked at his brother from under his eyelashes. "I can cook food at night and freeze it, have breakfast sandwiches in the freezer. You take all the jobs you need, brother."

Corinne looked over at Stretcher, who gave a slight nod. "Don't either one of you go changing your lives for me. I'm an imposition at best. Whatever you need to do to bring in the money, do it. Besides, I owe you for..."

Stretcher shook her head, James glared at her, and Mitch exploded. "You are recovering from one of the worst things that can happen to somebody. Do you think we would charge you for your recovery time?"

Stretcher blanched. "He didn't..." said Corinne.

"Betrayal," said James, quietly. "Bruises and bones heal. The sense of trust, not so much."

Stretcher sighed. "I don't think your mother would have seen it that way," she said, quietly. "There is a huge difference between stupidity and betrayal."

"Stretcher," said Mitch, his voice tight. "First, since it didn't happen to you, you've got no call talking about it with us. Second, Corinne is recovering, and she doesn't need to hear about any of this. How dare you bring it up with Corinne at this table?"

"Finish your pie," James said to Mitch. "Stretcher, you were out of line. Corinne, we apologize. I know you're curious as hell, but we'd like to ask you to keep that to a dull roar for now."

Stretcher spoke quietly. "I do apologize. You all are invited to a cookout this Friday afternoon. Just bring a sack of chips or something, a bottle of soda. You two are working hard and stretched thin. James, I happen to know you've got a fishing trip at oh-dark-thirty on Saturday morning. So, I suggest coming in separate trucks. Mitch and Corinne, you're invited to stay the night if you want. Everyone else is going to pitch tents in the backyard, as far away from the male goats as they can." James snorted. "You can have a recliner inside, Corinne. Rachael and Gunny feel really bad that this happened on the mountain behind them, and that nobody got up the mountain with the stretcher fast enough. We want to celebrate your recovery. Hell, we want to celebrate you, Blackie, and James making it down that mountain alive." Mitch looked thunderous, James thoughtful.

"So, your farm is at the base of the mountain, and that's why you were there to put me on the truck with the backboard?" asked Corinne.

James snorted. "That was the most improvised piece of shit I've ever seen in my damn life, but it worked. Rope, bungee cord, a travel pillow and a board. Was Gunny putting together a door or something?"

"Wardrobe," said Stretcher. "It was actually going to be one of the doors to Rachael's new wardrobe."

"Thank you," said Corinne. "If neither one of these two wants to go, can you have someone swing by and pick me up?"

James nodded slowly. "I'll come," he said quietly. He looked over at his brother. Mitch's jaw was clenched tightly, and tears filled his eyes. "Mitch, you don't have to go. If you can't be civil..."

Mitch unclenched his jaw, and nodded once. "I will act exactly the way our parents raised us to be."

"That's all anyone can ask," said Stretcher. "Gunny promises to stay on the other side of wherever you are. Rachael wants to see you more than anything, and she's cooking up quite a spread." Stretcher moved, and James let her out. She stood, threw some bills down on the table, and said in a very low voice, "We may have the most rude and bizarre family in the world, but you're still family."

Corinne finished her plate, pushed it into the middle of the table, and said, "You can cut this drama with a knife. Stretcher, I assume you guys are cousins or something."

"Or something," mumbled Mitch.

"But close enough," said James.

"Stretcher, I promise to keep these two in line. I'll carry a fork and stab either of them if they misbehave."

Stretcher smiled. "I bet you would, too. Don't worry. These boys like growling and snarling, but they're not so much on getting stabby. Tell you what. You stick by one, I'll stick by the other. Deal?"

"Deal," said Corinne. The two women shook, which raised James' eyebrows and made Mitch snarl. Stretcher gave a little bow of her head, then left with her fluid grace, long legs eating up the floor. She was outside in two seconds.

James sat back down. "We'll take a walk, but let us get back home first." Mitch nodded, James threw some bills down on the table, and then they walked back to the truck in complete silence. Corinne sat in the back, and reached forward with her good hand to touch Mitch's shoulder. His shoulder was so tight that it was a mess of knots. She dug into some of the knots with her thumb, and he groaned. He put his hand over hers, and kept his head down the whole ride.

# SECRET

$\mathcal{T}$hey got out of the truck, and Corinne leaned against it. "Somebody talk. I take it this Gunny person is ex-military, and that he's your dad or grandpa or something."

James pointed. "Let's walk. We'll be a lot cooler under the trees." Mitch nodded once, hard, and went inside his Harley garage to pound on a bike.

They took it super-slow on a nearly flat trail. James pulled up a picture on his cell phone, and handed it wordlessly to Corinne. Corinne knew who she was looking at without having to ask. The man had short brown hair, blue-green eyes, and a ready smile. He had given Mitch and James their noses, their high foreheads, the wrinkles on the corners of their eyes. Both men got their darker skin from their mom. Mitch had her mouth, and James had her high cheekbones.

"Dawn, part Pueblo native, part mestizo. She had me when she was eighteen and Mitch when she was nineteen. Poor woman had two wild boys back to back, and never stopped running. Our dad's name was Nick. The sweetest, most gentle guy in the world. They drove a truck together, until Mom got pregnant with me. Then they got a little cabin on this property, some hole in the wall without running water or flush toilets, and a packed wood floor. Heating was by a wood-burning stove, which my mother cooked on. My parents made the floor from logs they cut on this property. I was four when we got running water and indoor plumbing, six when Mom got her contractor's license. After that, she built a bedroom for each of us herself, installed the electrical. Eventually we moved in with Gunny and Rachael while she made the A-frame you see behind you. She worked on half the houses in this county. Got paid less than a man, until she made her own firm."

"So, normal, hard-working parents," said Corinne. "I'm taking it that the story doesn't end very well." James took Corinne on a flat path, covered with pine needles. They walked so slowly that they were almost standing still.

James sighed gustily. "No, it doesn't. I was thirteen and Mitch was twelve when mom fell off a ladder. Turned out she had a tumor in her brain. There was another one in her chest cavity. Sounds pretty obvious now that there was no way she was going to survive. But for Dad, there's no way in hell he would accept that."

"I'm sorry," said Corinne. "I had two normal, hard-working parents too, except for the fact that neither one of them gave a shit about me. Mom got some housekeepers and went to work until I turned about eight, then I took care of myself. Dad just never really came home from work. Physics professor. My mom's a lawyer with the empathy of a shark." She barked at a laugh. "Free college education, and that was it. Neither one of them came to graduation, any of them." She reached out, touched his shoulder. "I can't even imagine what it would be like to lose someone who actually loves you." She handed the phone back, and James pocketed it.

James swallowed, looked away, looked back. "It was really bad, in case you haven't figured that out. Our insurance was sort of piecemeal because of the truck driving and contracting, and there was a lot of shit the insurance companies didn't want to pay for. Dad did not want to constantly have to stop and start treatment, which he felt would kill her. He thought she was going to live. So, he got this crazy idea to join the military."

Corinne felt her stomach drop to her shoes. She reached out, took James' hand, and they walked hand-in-hand up the trail. She sighed. "He never came home," she said, as quietly as the pine needles falling.

"No, he didn't. He wasn't holding her when she died, he wasn't there to pick up the pieces. He died six days before she did in a helicopter accident. She kept asking for him, and we..."

Corinne stepped in front of James, slipped her arm out of the sling, and put her arms around him. He shook, and she felt the tears fall into her hair as he put his head on her shoulder. He stood, wiped them away from his cheeks. "We were taught never, ever to lie, that being honest and real was the most important thing that you could ever be and do. But we lied," he said, staring off into the woods, brushing his tears away. "We lied and told her that he was on a plane back, said it would only be a few more hours. She held on, in pain, waiting on him to show up, then slipped away in her sleep. I've never felt right about that lie, but Mitch just couldn't tell her, wouldn't let me tell her. Said she shouldn't die with a broken heart."

"Young boys watching their mothers die don't necessarily make the best decisions." Corinne touched his arm, then slid her bad arm back in its sling. "I take it he feels guilty about that? And so do you?"

"It was the wrong call," said James, simply.

"It was. But, your brother was right, too. She would've been so horribly worried about dying and leaving you alone."

"We weren't alone. We had Gunny, Rachael, Stretcher, Jared, the whole pack of them. She would have known that, and would know that we would be okay."

"Gunny did something wrong," reasoned Corinne. "Did he take the deaths wrong, take it out on you?"

James shook his head. "No, that wasn't it. You see, he also believed that Mama was going to live. Gunny is the one that encouraged my dad to sign up for the military. He suggested that dad join the Navy, said it would probably be the safest branch. He took Dad on long hikes, gave him difficult tasks to do like carrying rocks around in a rucksack so he would get through basic training. Worked, too, because my dad made it through basic training with no real problems.

Dad wasn't going into a war zone, said he would be fine. But they flew Dad out to the carrier, and he never came back. We begged him not to go. Mom said that it was his decision. Gunny stood by Dad, encouraged him. Said he'd be home safe and sound before we knew it."

"What a clusterfuck," said Corinne, stepping back and looking up into James' eyes.

James barked out a laugh. "Well, I've never heard it described that way, but that is kind of what happened."

"Your dad was trying to pay for your mom's treatment. Yes, he put himself in harm's way, but he did everything he could to come back to you."

"Oh, I don't blame Dad. He was trying to protect his wife. But Gunny, Gunny had other options. Rachael offered to put the farm in hock to pay for mom's treatment, said that whether she lived or died, anything was worth a fighting chance. Gunny and Dad were afraid that they would lose the farm, and Dad was a firm believer in cleaning up your own mess. For Gunny, it was about money. My mom's life was worth less than his farm."

"How many people lived on the farm at the time?" Corinne stopped walking, caught up in the story.

"Anywhere from six to eleven, depending on who was visiting from where." James' eyes widened. "Gunny was looking out for the farm people, and so was Dad."

"Clusterfuck," repeated Corinne. "There were absolutely no right options, what with everyone being so protective of everyone else. There was nothing that wouldn't get somebody badly hurt. The most horrible thing about all of this is that it was two little boys with no defense against any of this that paid the price." Corinne reached up and held James close with her good arm, her bad arm between them. He unbent and put his arms around her waist. "You paid a horrible price, and you have every right to be stone cold furious, but there were no good options for anyone in this situation. Everyone did the best they could and everyone fucked up badly. Let go of the anger, and keep the pain."

James stood back, and screamed out into the air. He sounded like an angry wolf, his arms wide, his head thrown back. He howled a second, then a third time. Corinne walked up to him, tapped him on the chest, and put her arms around him as he cried into her hair, her neck, and let his pain pour out of him.

He let go, stood back. "I've got to walk," he said, pointing down the trail. "Will you...?"

She turned, pointed back down the trail. "Can still see the house, moron." He barked out a laugh. "Go, do your mountain man hiking thing. I'll look after Mitch."

James' face grew still. "He took it hard."

"You both did. Now, get the hell out of here." She waved a hand in the direction of the trail. He nodded, turned, and started walking. But, Corinne noticed that he made sure that she had made it back to the house before he went around the bend at the top.

Corinne knew that what was teasing friendship had just gone around the bend to something...something more. James and Mitch were both...hot. James was more handsome, Mitch much rougher. They complemented each other. That heartbreaking story made her want to delve in, see what was in the quiet spaces of James' heart. Mitch...well, he needed to calm the hell down. Now she knew why he was wound so tight. Oddly, Mitch's very gruffness built her trust in him. No sappiness. James was attentive, and willing to do almost anything to help. But he recognized her space. Malcolm the Evil One never had.

Mitch was working on a bike, listening to music in his earphones so loudly that she could hear the song from the other side of the carport. It was, appropriately, "Cum On Feel The Noize." Corinne strode toward him, but he jerked his chin at the house. She flipped him off, and he flipped her off back. She turned, and strode back into the house. She came back out with Gatorade, the blue kind. She put it down just out of his reach, and he growled at her. She flipped him off again, and went back in to call Kandace, the only one of them in the same time zone. Corinne explained the situation to her friend, and Kandace said, "That situation sucks balls. How is anyone supposed to do the right thing, let alone have any idea of what the right thing was gonna be?"

"My sentiments exactly," Corinne reached down, got a can of Dr. Pepper out of her little refrigerator, and popped the top.

Kandace noticed it at once. "Your doctors say it's okay for you to go off the caffeine wagon?" Kandace had wanted to come over, but Corinne had told her to stay put. She'd waited until the nightmares had faded and she was well on the way to recovery to tell Kandace what was going on. She hadn't told Tania; their friend was scrambling, learning how to teach kids English in South Korea. Tania had no money to fly back anyway.

"No, not cleared for caffeine." Corinne sighed with pleasure at the first sip. "But it's either that or start behaving in a homicidal fashion, and these poor boys have been through enough without me being even worse." She groaned. "I've been a total witch to guys who lost their parents young."

"Did anyone tell you?"

"Not until just now."

"Then, there you go. Mitch is probably even more volcano-y than I was when I got sober. Do what you and Tania did for me."

"Good idea. I'll see if someone delivers. And installs."

Corinne searched online, found several choices that would deliver\, and ordered a full set. The brothers had a weight bench and weights, things with plates, on the back of the carport. The sporting goods store was absolutely delighted to come out and do a full installation on the carport ceiling. Corinne ordered a speed, heavy, and kickboxing bag trio, with same-day delivery and installation for a hefty fee.

Mitch stopped banging in his garage when the truck drove up. He saw what they were installing, grinned, and pointed out proper placement. He brought out a ladder for the carport ceiling install, and he also held the bags while they installed them. Corinne brought out cans of soda she'd stuffed in a bag, being one-handed, and found out the installers were local high school football team seniors. Mitch and Corinne shook their hands and sent them away.

Then, Corinne made Mitch install hooks for the various sets of gloves Corinne had ordered. "I take it the pink ones are mine?" he asked, holding them up. Corinne flipped him off again, and left him to beat the shit out of some bags. His muscles bunched, flowed. Corinne couldn't help it; she looked out the window from time to time, loving his tight ass and fierce intensity.

When it turned dark, Mitch came in and showered and they made sandwiches for dinner. James had not come back, but Mitch didn't seem to be concerned about that. "I take it he told you about the whole gory mess?"

"Mess is not the right term. I told your brother that it was a clusterfuck, and I stand by that terminology."

Mitch nodded, took two pickles, and shoved the jar over to Corinne. She took two, put the lid on, and put it back in the refrigerator. "Kind of sums it up." He took two slices of roast beef and put them on his sandwich. He put the roast beef away, and started on the ham.

"I can't begin to tell you how sorry I am that all that happened to you. My parents just don't know that I exist. Not in the same league at all."

"Funny. You don't seem to be invisible." Mitch put away the mustard and the bottle of garlic Parmesan dressing.

Corinne snorted. "My friends said the same thing. They told me to stay all the way through graduate school, that I might as well get my money's worth out of those a-holes. They were right. I learned how to do everything on the website, front end, back end, write the copy, one-stop service. And, I got a dual master's in web development and online business administration so I could run my own company."

She poured a bag of Cool Ranch Doritos into a bowl. "I've been thinking about cloud computing, but I want to stay here. I don't do websites because I'm lazy. Half the work I do is for nonprofits. I could do the whole Microsoft or Google thing, sleep under my desk for five years, work ninety hours a week, retire. But, this way I get actual free time. I know this sounds weird, but it's what I want."

Mitch and Corinne sat down at the table with their sandwiches and a can of Coke each. "It's not weird. I could've done the same damn thing, worked in a Harley store or garage. But, in case you haven't figured it out, I've got a problem with authority."

"No shit, Sherlock."

Mitch flipped her off. "I also have no urge to work sixteen hours a day. I like to work when I want to work, stop when I don't. We inherited this house, bought surrounding land because my brother and I don't have big needs. Yeah, we have a few video game consoles and we have the requisite big black TV." Corinne snorted. "What can I say? We're males." Corinne grinned. "But give me a bike, regular food like sandwiches and hot dogs, a garage, and a house like this, and I'm pretty happy. There was a forest fire here a few years back, burned out some houses of people who really couldn't afford to lose everything. James got them out, and we both did volunteer firefighting. We're both trained. We made sure those people got the money to start over, have a new life, and we got a new life too. We run a risk staying up here, if it gets too dry. But, this is our home."

"Do you think your mom and dad would've liked it? What you've done with the place, what you've done with your lives. Because I do."

"Not ready to talk about them. Or Gunny, or any of the rest of them. We were relying, I was relying on them to make better decisions. And yes, I know they were damn few options in the first place, and all of them were bad. They didn't make the right ones, and my brother gave up hoops, football, everything to be sure everything was good with me. Did you know that he was going to join the military? Become an officer, see the world? Get paid to get any damn degree he wanted? But, he didn't do that, because it would've left me with absolutely no one if he had gotten himself killed. Couldn't be a cop either, same reason." Mitch looked off into space, then back at Corinne. "Stop looking at me with those damn cow eyes. I survived, we survived. Eat your damn sandwich and shut up."

"These are not cow eyes. I do not make cow eyes at people." She threw a chip at him. "Shut up and eat your damn food, you freak." Mitch grinned at her, and ate his sandwich.

# COOKOUT

They took two vehicles to the cookout. James helped Corinne into Mitch's truck. James had all sorts of fishing gear in the back, including waders. "Fishing trip with high school buddies," he explained. "I'll be gone for days after this."

Mitch said, "It would be good to get him out of the way." James shut Corinne's door, came around the truck, and punched his brother in the arm. He then got into his own truck and led the way down and around the mountain.

Corinne recognized the mountain and cringed a bit. She had talked to the police several times, but nobody knew where Malcolm was, and now he had even more of a reason to disappear. He had been fired from his Boston job after his first week because he wanted to tell stories rather than code, and he'd been staying in a hotel before going to see Corinne. Malcolm was in the wind.

Corinne sighed, and let it go. She'd tightened up the straps on her sling, and had begun kickboxing again. She did everything in slow motion so she didn't jostle the arm, but she was determined to get herself in shape again. Mitch knew and supported her. James didn't, and would have had a cow. James was very protective of Corinne, and Corinne loved it deep inside in some core she didn't know she had.

No one had wanted to protect her before, except for her crazy-ass female friends.

Mitch was absolutely silent on the drive, and played rock music so loudly Corinne couldn't hear herself think. Since Mitch obviously didn't have thinking in mind, she decided not to say anything and just enjoy the ride. Corinne vaguely recalled the mountain's base where she had shown up, so damaged, at the bottom. She wondered where the big black and gray wolf-dog was, then decided not to worry about anything. She was going to have enough trouble making sure Mitch didn't have a meltdown, and that James didn't withdraw into himself. She sang along to Def Leppard's "Pour Some Sugar on Me," and let the mountain air slap her face on the way down.

Corinne opened the door with her arm and foot and used the grab bar to lower herself down before Mitch could get all the way around the truck. James rushed up to her, glared down at her with his arms crossed and said, "What the hell do you think you're doing?"

Corinne smiled sweetly up at him. "Did you get the memo? I'm rather self-destructive." She shut the door of the truck with her good arm, and winced as she jostled her bad shoulder.

James glared at her again. "Woman, now you're self-injuring just to spite me. Get over your special self."

Corinne stuck her tongue out at him. "Classy," noted Mitch. He leaned back his head, sniffed the air. "I smell cow. And pig." He grabbed the bag of chips in one hand and a two-liter in the other, and marched toward the source of the food.

"Rachael usually does the steaks, because Gunny usually chars some on the outside and leaves them raw on the inside. He's safe enough." James held out his hand, palm flat. "I would suggest inside the house. There are citronella candles everywhere, so the mosquitoes won't bite, but it's cooler in there. Besides, women like that sort of thing."

Corinne walked beside him as he trudged up the gravel drive past the trucks. SUVs, and jeeps in every color streaked with mud parked in long rows in the gravel parking lot. "What, air conditioning?"

"No, looking inside other people's houses. I think you all had training as spies, or else why would you like to look at other people's stuff?"

Corinne belted out a laugh. "Not so far from the truth." The door had a Spanish arch, and over the arch was a moon tile sculpture, black with a moon inlay, not the usual southwestern moon-and-sun. James reached past her and opened the door. Inside, there were soft gold tile floors, light blue walls, and ice-cold air conditioning. Corinne went in, and shut the door quickly behind her. She sighed deeply. "You're right, girls do like air-conditioning." James laughed.

A man the approximate size of a house was in the kitchen cutting things at the huge breakfast bar topped with gray granite. There was a deep farm sink, a stove with six electric burners, and a huge side-by-side refrigerator in silver behind him. "James," his voice boomed. "Heard you were coming. Anyone want to help me with the salsa? Except you, Corinne. I saw your body when they loaded you up a couple weeks back. Don't think your arm will hold up."

James groaned, but took quick strides toward the kitchen. "Don't dare her, Gunny, or she'll show you you're wrong by hurting herself."

Gunny boomed out a laugh. His hair was cut in a very short buzz cut, the same caramel color as his eyes and skin. "I seem to remember quite a few broken bones on your part over the years," he said, gesturing with the chef's knife. "Take a load off at the breakfast bar, Corinne. We men will cry over the onions." Corinne headed for the tall but comfortable black barstools with backs. James reached out with a hand on her good side to help her up.

"Screw the onions," said James. "Give me some of those green chiles." Gunny boomed out more laughter, and passed James a cutting board, paring knife, can of green chilies, and can opener. James opened the can, saved the juice from the can in a little bowl he pulled out of the cabinet, slipped on gloves that were on the counter, and started dicing the chiles.

"Corinne, you did a great job on our website," said Gunny. "The crafts page is doing great. We've got people from all over the valley selling things there. Roberto sold six paintings last week."

"What Gunny isn't telling you is that Roberto has only one arm, and is paralyzed on the other side of his body. He does everything with one arm and one foot."

"Good Lord above," said Corinne. "You must think of me as the biggest slacker ever."

Gunny roared out another laugh, then he got serious. "You held off an attacker a head bigger than you, got yourself to safety, popped your arm in by yourself, and were headed down before that big..."

"Wolf-dog," supplied James. "Named Blackie."

Gunny's cough sounded suspiciously like a laugh. "Anyway, you did it yourself. And we're damn proud of you for it." He snaked a giant arm behind James to the refrigerator, opened it, popped the top, and passed Corinne a Dr. Pepper.

Corinne sighed, and looked at Gunny lovingly. "My hero," she said in a sappy voice. Gunny roared out more laughter.

The salsa took shape, with tomatoes, slivers of red onion, and green chilies. Gunny handed a mango to James, and said, "Use your mother's recipe. She made the best mango salsa anywhere."

"I'd like that," said James. "Use one of those gorilla arms and get me some limes."

Gunny barked out more laughter, and handed James two limes from out of the refrigerator. "Your aunt Rachael made key lime pie, apple, and plum pie too."

"Good God," said James. "Your woman is gonna make me so fat that they have to roll me back up the mountain."

"Wait until you taste your steak with chimichurri sauce," said Gunny. "Woman also can make a mean baked potato, fully loaded. I absolutely know that we are going to run out of sour cream."

"You make enough tortillas?" asked James. "We ran out last time."

"Dogs. We all eat like dogs. Or wolves."

James roared out a laugh. "That we do, Gunny. That we do."

They made Corinne in charge of taking one bowl at a time out to the giant table in the backyard, really several long white plastic tables laid out end-to-end, covered with a red-and-white checkered plastic tablecloth, with white plastic folding chairs and benches all around. Corinne brought out three kinds of salsa—mango, pico de gallo, and Diablo made with three kinds of hot peppers. She brought out three plastic nested bowls with three different bags of chips in them, opened them with her teeth, and dumped the chips into each bowl.

She went back in, and sat down. "I think it's at least ten degrees hotter out there than it is at the top of the mountain. I nearly got licked to death by a golden retriever, until the German shepherd protected me."

Both Gunny and James laughed. "I'm afraid the golden retriever is named Goldie, which is so damn typical it makes me cry," said Gunny, pretending to wipe tears from his eyes. "The German Shepherd's name is Shadow. Jared is that really tall guy helping Rachael with the steaks and potatoes who helped get you down the mountain and into the ambulance. He managed to get his dog home from overseas. Jared and the dog now work search and rescue, find lost hikers. They found a little six-year-old boy last week, so today he gets all the steak he wants, within reason. The dog, I mean. The man can put away steak too."

"Goldie doesn't get anything," warned James. "And she will beg you, pretend that she has never eaten before in her whole, entire fat dog life. Everyone has to take extra walks with her because she's such a pig when she visits."

Rachael came in, a curvy woman with long black hair, caramel eyes and skin, a round face, and a huge smile,. She kissed Gunny, gave James an enormous hug, and touched Corinne's good shoulder. "I am so glad my boys got you off the mountain," she said, smiling at Corinne.

Gunny let out a grunt, and James said, "She means me and Blackie. The wolf-dog."

Rachael let out a peal of laughter. She took off her apron, hung it up, and took out several large knives and serving forks. "You boys better finish with that salad," she said. Gunny cut corn off the cob, and James cut up red bell peppers into cubes. "Or, that steak won't be there for you." She grinned at Corinne. "Don't be chopping off any fingers in your hurry," as Gunny and James began moving their hands much more quickly. "Come along, dear," she said to Corinne. "Have you ever had steak tacos with chimichurri sauce?"

"No," said Corinne, as Rachael wrapped her arm in Corinne's good arm. "But I think that will probably be happening in the next five minutes."

Rachael laughed. "I like you," she said, her eyes bright. "And I hear that you promised to run interference with the boys. James seems to be doing very well."

"I think he figured some things out."

"Then you'd better sit by Mitch. Boy's stewing in his own juices." Rachael expertly passed out the serving forks and spoons among the various bowls and platters.

"He should be exhausted after beating the snot out of the kick-boxing equipment I got him."

"Oh, my. You're good for my boys, aren't you?" Rachael put the fingers of her good hands to her lips and let out an ear-piercing whistle. Everyone, dogs included, stopped what they were doing and rushed toward the table from both inside and outside the house.

"Damn. Bet no one ignores you."

Rachael looked over at Corinne. "Anyone who ignores you is a fool," she said, in a low voice. "Sit here," she said, pointing to her left. "Keep you from getting jostled."

Mitch came over and sat down next to Corinne. He nodded at Rachael, and Corinne took his hand. Mitch held onto Corinne's hand, and shocked the hell out of her by kissing her cheek. "What was that for?" she asked quietly.

Mitch whispered into Corinne's ear. "Mine," he said, quietly. "When the firefighters, rescue squad, and paramedics sit down, I don't want you looking at them. I want you to look at me."

Corinne tried very hard not to gasp. "What about fishing guides?"

"That one's okay," said Mitch, his breath warm on her ear. "But no one else."

Corinne struggled to keep track of the names. Ricardo was the fireman, who everyone called Rico. Luce was the paramedic, Yancey a cop, and obviously ex-military like Stretcher. It turned out Stretcher did some cyberspace thing, something to do with nondisclosure agreements. Corinne suspected it was either banking or government. Frank and Paul, who everyone called Pete and Repeat, were sandy-haired twins with stubbly beards, both search and rescue. Paul was Goldie's dad, and Jared was the dog Shadow's partner.

Sylvie had elvin features with a pointed chin, high cheekbones, and huge limpid brown eyes, and had everyone wrapped around her little finger. Corinne was stunned as Sylvie made highly insightful comments in a piping voice the entire time. Maybelle, Sylvie's mother, was as thin as a bird and just as flighty, her nervous hands smoothing tablecloths and red-checkered paper napkins. Her entire face was pulled forward like a dog's, and her eyes were nearly black.

Rachael stood, and the table grew silent. Everyone stood up, and Rachael sang a prayer in rapid Spanish, something about spirit and life. Everyone lowered their heads and said "Amen," including Corinne, and then everyone talked at once as they passed the food around.

Mitch spent the entire time talking to Corinne, with occasional comments toward Rachael. He did speak to Rachael in a very respectful tone. Mitch was jumpy and dissatisfied, but he ate all his tacos. James sat on the other end of the table near Rico and Gunny, and exchanged jokes that had everyone at that end of the table doubled over with laughter. Corinne noticed Gunny hesitantly put his hand on James' shoulder, and James smiled back at him. Corinne smiled, and dug into the best tacos she'd ever eaten in her life.

Mitch seemed to relax in increments. He listened to firefighter and paramedic stories about daring rescues and talked about the motorcycles he'd built and sold. He also talked about trails he and James had blazed that summer. He talked about hiking in the woods, the camping gear left behind, the idiocy of hunters. Hunters were not allowed on the mountain, because it was protected land. They could hunt in the next county over, with certain licenses. They could fish in the rivers, because they were deep. Mitch had rather denigrating terms for a lot of the hunters, saying that they often couldn't see an orange vest if it were directly in front of them.

Corinne butted in more than once to keep Mitch's attention on her and not on Gunny at the other end of the table. Rachael also threw in comments from time to time, designed to distract the firefighters and trailblazers from more risqué talk. Gunny's booming voice came out over everything, and more than once he referred to "Mitchie," which made Mitch stiffen, his face growing dark. Rachael actually got up from the table, whacked Gunny upside the head with two fingers, and said something in his ear. After that, there were no more references to "Mitchie."

Corinne was happy to see James relax completely, crack jokes, shove on shoulders, and generally act as if he were having a very good time. Mitch looked over at his brother and got a very dark look in his eyes more than once. Corinne touched Mitch's hand and said, "Mitch, why haven't you chopped anything off with that axe? You seem to be swinging it around way too much." Mitch turned bright red, everyone around him started cracking jokes about the size of his manhood, and Mitch quit thinking about his brother for quite some time.

The pies came out, and everyone descended upon them like a pack of wolves. They were cut into slivers so everyone could have all the types of pie, passed out, and gone within minutes. Corinne shuddered with joy. The key lime pie had been made from real key limes, the apple pie was mostly apples with a touch of cinnamon and brown sugar, and the peach pie tasted like biting into a fresh peach.

Cleanup literally took minutes. Everyone stood almost a complete arm's length away, and passed the empty dishes down in a line from picnic table to the back patio door. There was literally no food left on the table.

# FAMILY

*A*fter the picnic, Corinne dragged Mitch inside. Corinne took her arm out of the sling and rinsed the dishes while Mitch filled up the dishwasher and turned it on. Then, they hand-washed the serving plates. Each pot had already been cleaned and scrubbed as it was used and emptied. Gunny stayed outside with James and cleaned the grill.

Rachael and Stretcher dried the serving dishes, and Rico worked with Stretcher to put everything away. Rachael kept touching Mitch, his shoulder, his hand, and passed him dry dish towels. Corinne put her arm back in the sling, then cut her eyes at Stretcher. "Stretcher, can you give me a tour of this place?"

Stretcher literally grabbed her healed hand and pulled her away from the kitchen. "Living room," she said unnecessarily, as the place was filled with long black couches, two black recliners, little tables for drinks and snacks, an enormous wide-screen TV that took up almost the entire wall, and a console with various game systems underneath, controllers on chargers. "Laundry room," said Stretcher, and unloaded the dryer, filled it up with wet sheets from the washer and turned it on, filled up the washer, and turned it on as well. Stretcher carried the full laundry basket down the hall and Corinne followed.

Corinne had an impression of a narrow girl's room with bunk beds and shelves full of books, walls in shades of lavender and blue. That was probably Sylvie's room, with a room next to it done up in pink, blue, and white, an old-fashioned quilt on the four-poster bed. That would be Sylvie's mama's room. There was a bathroom with three separate sinks, a long shower that could hold two people, and a fat bathtub. A little farther down there were bedrooms that were obviously inhabited by males, laundry overflowing from laundry baskets but surprisingly picked up. There were maps of the county, sports detritus such as baseballs and soft basketball hoops with trash cans underneath, e-book readers strewn on beds.

Halfway down the hall, Stretcher dragged Corinne into a room. There was a queen-sized bed with drawers underneath, shelves with fat mathematics textbooks on them, more county maps on the walls, a wardrobe with an open door that had everything from jeans to leathers, and in the corner was a simple black lacquer locked case. On top was a *katana* and *wakizashi* set, the double Japanese swords in black sheaths with silver and black wraps on the handles, the set simple and unadorned. They were on a stand that had obviously been mended. The other wall held a metal table with a shockproof laptop. Two screens hung on the wall, and the wires were carefully corralled. Stretcher acted as if her room wasn't on the Zen side, poured out the contents of the basket, handed to ends to the soft black sheet to Corinne, and took the other end. "Someone told you what the hell is going on," said Stretcher. "Was it James or Mitch?"

"James told me about the clusterfuck," said Corinne.

Stretcher burst out a coughing laugh, folded the sheet lengthwise, then started walking towards Corinne to fold the sheet again. "That's the best way of describing what the hell happened that I've ever heard. Everyone tried to do their best, but no one knew what the hell the right thing was, and no one could have foreseen a training accident. Everyone's been a hot mess. The boys got out of this house as quickly as they could, the day James turned eighteen. Mitch declared himself emancipated, and moved in with his brother the same day. We all saw it coming, kind of like a train wreck we couldn't stop. It was absolutely nothing anyone could say to get those two boys to stop blaming Gunny, and since Gunny blamed himself, they all just kind of bought into it."

Stretcher put the folded sheet down, pulled out another one. Corinne grabbed the ends on one side. "Gunny was wrong, but Nick was a grown man who made his own decisions. I think no one knew what to do with two hurt, grieving boys who never really grew past losing both their parents at once."

"Would you?" asked Stretcher.

"I don't know. My parents never really noticed I existed. I took their money, went all the way through grad school, earned degrees in web design, business, and English for the copywriting. Did some internships, one at a big company, and a little startup, hated them both. Decided I would either do business by myself, or not do it. I have ADD, so working by myself makes the most sense. I can work any time I want, take all the breaks I need, work on two projects at the same time or back to back, and still get everything done the right way."

Stretcher nodded. "I'm your standard throwaway. Same shit, different day. Had asthma, outgrew that, learned more by doing than by studying. Then there's the lesbian thing. That one was the last straw. Out on my ear at fifteen."

"How did you end up here?" asked Corinne. They folded one more sheet, then started on the pillowcases.

"Everyone knows about Gunny and Rachael. They take in certain kids, the really different ones." She cut her eyes over to Corinne. "Do you know how different Mitch and James are?"

"Let me see," said Corinne. "You can't get them inside unless it's to bolt down food, which they eat constantly. They are always outside or on the mountain. They can stay still for a certain amount of time, then they're gone. They're highly intelligent, very funny, with a wicked sense of humor, both of them. I haven't seen a single photo of their parents in the house, or any other family except the two of them, and then only one or two shots on the refrigerator. They're definitely not vegetarian, they're extremely protective, and they don't hesitate at saving lives. Of course, there may be more than one person living in the mountains that are like this. Loners are kind of a category all to themselves." *Wow, I've been paying more attention than I thought.*

Stretcher snorted, and coughed out another laugh. "Let me make a recommendation to you, Corinne. You seem like an extremely strong and good person. You're certainly able to defend yourself in a fight, you don't hesitate at doing what needs to be done, and you're really good with both of them. You also seem to be kind of a loner too. I know both of them are attracted to you, because I can smell it, it's in their eyes, the set of their jaws. Mitch is a bit possessive, but the minute you say the word no he'll be across the room, even out the door. James will literally do anything for anyone, and will hand over his heart. Are you sleeping with either one of them?"

Corinne nearly dropped the pillowcase she had been holding. "What the...No! And how is that any of your business?"

"They both are falling in love you. You're strong enough for either one of them. But, you need to have a little talk with both of them before anything starts. This family is very special, protective of its members. I can't say that I would kill you if you hurt either one of them, because one of them is going to get hurt when you make your choice. But, whichever one you choose, if you hurt that one, all bets are off."

Corinne sat down on the bed, and stared at the wall washed with gold. The wall seemed to gleam from the inside. "What kind of paint did you use to get the metallic sheen?" she asked quietly.

"ADD," said Stretcher. "It's a special blend. And, spray paint mixed with glossy indoor paint."

"Squirrel," said Corinne, looking off to the side. This was an old ADD joke, referring to the tendency of dogs to pay attention—until they saw a squirrel. Both women chuffed laughter. "I love them both, because James is on a life-saving thing, came to get me and take me home, both of them looking out for me every day for the past three weeks. Hell, today, Mitch cut up my food again. Makes me feel like a damned six-year-old, but my shoulder is nowhere near healed yet. Still really sore." *Wait, did I say love instead of care about?* She stared blankly at the golden wall, trying to focus her thoughts. "It's in the thousand little things they do. James brought me chocolate with toffee chunks. Love that stuff. Mitch changes my sheets every two days. Says I can't get all funky. He folds my shirts exactly the way I like them. They do a thousand little things, and I can't even explain it."

"I can. They're mating with you."

"Now you've gone crazy. We're just friends. Hell, I didn't even know James before he walked me down the mountain."

"Bonding experience." Stretcher folded the last two pillowcases. She put all of the bedding in a pile, opened the middle drawer under her platform bed, put them in, and shut the door.

"You're out of your damn mind. And isn't at least one of the boys in this house gay?"

"Rico. He's the firefighter, in love with a paramedic from the next county over. So, we usually don't see him, except the big barbecue things. This one we held in your honor. We've seen the looks in their eyes, the way they protect you, treat you. We wanted to get to know you better."

"Well, I'm bright, I work damn hard to get what I've got, and apparently I surround myself with lunatics. Now, if you'll excuse me, Mitch should have had enough time with Rachael to behave a little bit better." Corinne opened up the door, went out and down the hall looking for Mitch, but found the kitchen completely empty. "Oh, shit."

Stretcher came out, looked around. "You got that right." She lunged toward the kitchen door, and went outside, Corinne on her heels.

The yard was deadly silent. Gunny had his hands out, and moved to put them behind his back. James came out of nowhere to hold Mitch's arm as Mitch aimed his fist toward Gunny's face. Corinne couldn't move quite as quickly, but she ran over, hissing as she shook her injured shoulder with each footfall. Without thinking, she got in between Mitch and Gunny. "Mitch, you've got reasons to be pissed, but this is a family barbecue. You want to be an ass, do it in private." She made her voice low and cutting, sure to grab his attention.

"You'll want to move now," said Mitch, his voice low.

"Hell I will. You got no call attacking a grown man at a family barbecue. What are you? Six?" She reached up on her tiptoes and tapped his forehead, letting heat show in her eyes. "Now get your ass in the truck. I need someone to take me home."

"The woman wants you to do something," said James. "I bet her arm's real sore after today. I think we should take her home."

Corinne wasn't above a little manipulation. She put a little of her real pain into her eyes, and held her arm very carefully as if it were glass.

"Well, shit," said Mitch. He reached down, gently took her good shoulder, and steered her toward the truck. He took two steps, looked back, and said, "Gunny, this isn't over." To his credit, Gunny stood there with his hands behind his back, and nodded once.

Corinne genuinely tripped, her eyes not on her feet but at the drama going on behind her. She hissed, and said, "Eyes, Corinne. Look where you're frigging going."

James snorted. Somehow, he was right by her side. "You know the ADD thing means you need to focus, don't you?"

Corinne slugged his arm. "Idiot," she said quietly.

James huffed out laughter, then rushed to open the door to get her into Mitch's truck. He handed her up, careful not to brush her bad arm. "You two behave," he said, putting a little bit of a smile in his voice.

"Glad to see you're all chummy," said Mitch, a very ugly tone in his voice. "Go ahead, stay over."

"I will," said James, his voice light. "I've got to get to bed early because I have a four ay em pickup for some fishing."

Mitch snarled. "Asshole," said Corinne, and she slugged his shoulder with her good hand. "Gunny's not saying he didn't fuck up. But, your daddy was a grown man, and made a grown man's decision for his family. Gunny couldn't have stopped him if he really wanted to go."

Mitch started to snarl, and realized he would be snarling at Corinne. He closed his mouth with an audible click of his teeth. He clenched his jaw, turned on the truck, and pulled out, as James jumped back. Corinne punched Mitch's arm again, and said, "You damn near ran over your brother. You will apologize when he gets home. Now, take me home, and you better not jostle my damn shoulder. It hurts."

"Bossy," said Mitch, through clenched teeth.

"You act like a two-year-old, you get treated like one. You've got the child's grief and anger, but none of the adult nuance. Put yourself in your daddy's shoes, making the completely impossible decisions he was trying to make. He was trying to provide for his family, and you know damn well he had to take care of that."

"James shouldn't have said a damn thing to you. This was our private stuff."

"He had to, or I would've stuck my foot where it doesn't belong, in my mouth," Corinne shot back. "I don't have enough filters because of the ADD, and that kind of clusterfuck past you all have is like a mine-field. Your brother didn't want me setting off bombs. But, it seems you planted your own damn grenades. Quit throwing them at me." Mitch gusted off a sigh, and they spent the rest of the drive in clench-jawed silence.

# PETULANCE

$\mathcal{M}$itch got out of the truck, ran around, and angrily opened Corinne's door. Corinne took his hand and hopped out, and hissed when she landed a little rough. She sighed and walked toward the house. Mitch slammed the truck door, then instead of running ahead of Corinne and opening the door like he usually did, he turned and headed to the woodpile. He stripped off his shirt, grabbed a chunk of wood, grabbed his axe, hefted it, and slung it down to cleanly slice a piece of wood in two. Corinne stood there a minute, and watched the interplay of muscles under skin turned dark from the sun. Corinne decided that he was a grown man and didn't need a babysitter, used the house key under the wheel well of the truck, unlocked the door, put the key back, and went into the house.

The house was blessedly cool, but strangely silent after the hours spent listening to the talk and laughter of other people. Corinne actually had no urge to come back to the house. She had been enjoying the family atmosphere, the closeness, the jokes, the camaraderie. She was pissed at Mitch for screwing it up, but understood why. She pulled up a nearly finished website and banged out a landing page for a social media ad. She got the fonts and colors just right, emailed the client to specify that the ad should run exactly as she had it laid out, double-checked everything, then sent the ad to be verified. She tested several new ads, added photos of officers to an About Me page for a client, and got up to grab some Mountain Dew.

While she was working, Mitch had gone from cutting wood to banging around, rattling wrenches and moving things with far more force than he needed to. Eventually, Corinne realized that she hadn't heard from Mitch in a while. She grabbed her soda, then checked the workshop, the woodpile, and kickboxing equipment. But, he was gone, and his truck was still there. The mosquitoes were out, and she was very glad that she had put on insect repellent before going to the picnic. The sun had already set, and Corinne looked out into the gloaming. She couldn't see Mitch at all. She called for him from all four sides of the house, even whistled, but he didn't come. He had always come when she called.

Corinne fought the first traces of nervousness. She made herself a small sandwich, not very hungry after the enormous amount she'd eaten for lunch. She checked both inside and outside the house again as darkness fell into a star-spangled cobalt. An hour later, she was getting nervous. She tried working on something, reading an ebook, putting together the social media marketing course she was designing, even watching some very bad television, but Mitch still hadn't come home. She circled the house again, called Mitch's name, but there was no one out there. *Apparently, I love that asshole enough to miss him,* she thought to herself. But the unease wouldn't go away.

Corinne called James. She explained the situation to him tersely, and said, "It's pitch black out there, except for the moonlight. I'm not quite so stupid to go wandering around in the dark with the messed-up arm, but I'm getting worried."

James said, "I know it's hard to believe this, but I think he's perfectly fine, and I think I know where he's gone. I am pissed as hell about his leaving you, but you should be fine where you are. Do not leave the house. Don't worry. We know these mountains like we know our fingers and toes. Mitch does too."

Corinne looked out the big picture window, and saw a dark shape with triangular ears out in the darkness. "Blackie."

James let out a small laugh. "I know this is even harder for you to believe, but if Blackie's there, trust me, Mitch is fine. Go on out. I bet Blackie wants to see you. I'm sorry, I've got to go, we're going on a night hike. See you in a few days." The phone went dead in Corinne's hand.

Corinne pocketed her cell phone, and started when Blackie let out a howl like his heart was breaking. She grabbed a Mountain Dew out of the refrigerator, went outside, and sat down on the front porch. She popped the top. Before she had time to register his presence, Blackie was on the porch, snuffling her hand. She sat down in the Adirondack chair. Blackie hopped up on the little table in between the two chairs and snuffled her neck, making Corinne laugh. The big wolf-dog laid his head down on her lap. Corinne stroked the massive head, laughed as Blackie licked her elbow.

The wolf-dog twisted his head when she scratched behind each ear, and looked up at her with doleful eyes. "I think we've got some chicken, if you're hungry." Blackie stood up, then carefully sat down. Corinne laughed, then left the wolf-dog there when she went inside to grab the half chicken that was still left. She put it on a pie plate and carried it out to the wolf-dog. He snapped it up as soon as the plate was on the ground. He finished it, then lay down to work on the bones. Corinne sat down again on a low Adirondack chair, resumed sipping her Mountain Dew.

Blackie went over, and lay down on her feet, snapping down the last of the chicken bones. He let out a belch, a little fart, and a small howl, making Corinne laugh. Blackie went around the house, did his business, and came back. He climbed up on the deck and put his massive head back on her lap. She stroked his fur, a combination of soft and coarse. The dog closed his eyes in absolute joy and happiness.

Somehow Corinne managed to fall asleep out there, exhausted from the day fraught with tension, meeting everyone, and diverting Mitch from a fight. She woke up, hand on Blackie's neck, and realized that his fur was getting shorter. In a moment, it was Mitch, naked as the day he was born, his head in Corinne's lap. Corinne had no idea why she didn't get up and scream, or start running. It may have been exhaustion, waking from a deep sleep, or that some part of her knew that Mitch and Blackie were the same person. Wolf. Were-something. Whatever. She was, however, unable to speak as Mitch sat up, stretched, popped his back, and grinned insouciantly at Corinne.

Corinne finally found her voice. "You are an asshole, and you still owe your brother an apology." She put her good hand on her hip, and narrowed her eyes at him. "And go put some damn clothes on, you idiot. Rude werewolf."

"We're shapeshifters, not weres," said Mitch, affronted. "My mama could turn into three kinds of wolf, and my dad two kinds of dog, a coyote, and a really small hyena. Since hyenas aren't native to here, Dad assumed that we're also part African-American somewhere in our family tree."

"You're still a naked asshole. Get some damn pants on. Just because you saved me from a horrible mountain death doesn't mean you can get away with bad manners."

"Bossy."

"You call me that again, you're gonna start losing body parts." Mitch laughed and went into the house. Once the door closed behind them, Corinne put her head in her hands. "Tania and Kandace are going to come back and stick me in a funny farm if I say any of this out loud," Corinne said to herself.

"You just did," yelled Mitch, from inside the house.

"You are so dead." Corinne stood up and stretched, feeling her back and neck pop. "I would kill you if I weren't so damn tired."

"Promises, promises." Mitch stuck his head out. He was wearing blue shorts and absolutely nothing else. He looked as good as choco- late mint ice cream ready to be licked. "You coming to bed?"

Corinne knew damn well he didn't mean her bed in the guestroom. Just for a moment the sadness that lay under his rage kicked up into his eyes. His shoulders slumped forward just a bit, and Corinne saw the teenager who had lost both his parents in horrible ways. She stepped forward. Without thinking, she kissed his cheek, then put her arms around him. He looked at her, took her face in his hands, smiled down at her, and kissed her lips. At first the kiss was light, barely pressing of his lips into hers, then it turned darker, deeper. She didn't know whether or not to continue or push away as the dark kiss hit her like a hammer.

Mitch turned out to be a shapeshifter, a man who had lost his parents, secrets upon secrets, revealed to her. James and now Mitch had given her their trust, something she had never received before in her entire life. Her parents entrusted her to be alone, only because they had no idea that a seven-year-old should not be left alone. They entrusted her to do her homework by herself, because it never occurred to them that she might need help with that. She realized that except for her sister-friends, every single time she thought someone had trusted her they were actually neglecting her. Until now.

And trust was the basis for love.

She found herself responding, her body in love with not just his delicate fingers, his abs rock-hard against her sling, the way he looked at her that broke her heart. She instinctively knew that rejection at this point would harm him in ways that may take years to recover. She had hauled out and seen all of his secrets, and she sincerely doubted anyone else did, except for family. Corinne felt a tiny spike of jealousy at the thought of a young Mitch fumbling with the girl behind the bleachers, or kissing another hiker out on the trails, sleeping with some woman in a tent. She wondered why the hell her mind was doing its ADD skipping-like-a-stone thing, but then realized it was because of the complete and total passion that he was pouring into his lips, and now his tongue, questing into her mouth. And the shapeshifter thing, but that one would just make her spin for days.

*Shut up, Corinne,* she screamed at herself and her own mind. *Just, for once. Shut. Up.* She ignored the ranting in her brain, let her thoughts flow in the wind like dandelion fluff, reached around his body with her one good arm, slid a hand down his back. He hissed into her mouth, surprised.

He pulled back, and they both gasped. "Be sure," said Mitch, his forehead on hers, his lips whispering into her mouth, fingers caressing her hair. "Please, please be sure. If you say no..."

"Then you'll jump backwards off the porch. Then you'll break your shoulder, so we can be winged twins." He guffawed a laugh. "Let's start with tonight," she said into his mouth.

"Tonight," he agreed.

Corinne kicked off her sandals just inside the door. Mitch shut the door, then led her up the stairs, holding her hand so she wouldn't fall off the rail-less side of the wooden planks hanging in the air all up the back wall, to the king-size bed in his room. She knew there were king-sized beds in both rooms, having very carefully gone up the stairs to bring the laundry back down in a sack she put on her back, one of the few chores they would let her do. She would know Mitch's room anywhere. There were little miniature Harleys on floating shelves all along one wall. There was another flat-screen TV, and wireless game controllers on the left side of the platform bed tables, sticking out like wings. There was a handcrafted pot on another floating shelf done in Zuni designs, black and white and yellow. The walls were hewn wood that seemed to glow inside from having been polished and sealed.

There was an en suite bathroom with the requisite bar of Lava soap on the left-hand side of the blue-and-gold pebbled glass sink and a small white fingernail brush, ready for him to try to scrub the grease out from under his fingernails from working on Harleys all day. The shower didn't surprise her. The separate enormous soaking tub did. Mitch shared the bathroom with his brother, so maybe the bath was for James, soaking out days of heat or cold on the trails.

Corinne had to rein in her stuttering thoughts again, but lost them as she unstrapped her sling, one strap at a time, with fumbling fingers. Mitch stilled her hands, and expertly guided the straps out very, very carefully. He got the sling off, set it to the side, put her good hand through the shirt, pulled the top off overhead, and gently threaded her arm out of the shirt. Corinne held her arm close, and sat down on the bed. He propped up pillows, and gently laid her back. She lay her bad arm on her stomach, and he looked at her, his eyes bright with hunger. He kissed her forehead, her eyes, nose, lips, ears. His kisses went down her collarbone. He spent time on each breast, making her arch her back, her bad arm folded under her breasts. She came with his attention to each breast, making him laugh in delight. Then, he carefully put her sling back on. Confused, Corinne said, "Was that it?"

Mitch laughed. "No, love, but I seem to be a bit undone. I would greatly prefer to leave you intact so we have the possibility of sex on some other night, and I can only do that if have the visual reminding me of the injury."

"Oh," she said. "Good." She raised her ass up into the air as he pulled off her panties and shorts. He spent time caressing her from her stomach on down, giving her butterfly kisses from her belly button, to her hips, inside of her thighs, all the way down to her ankles. He kissed back up inside of her thighs, making her gasp. He spent a lot of time kissing, touching, pushing on her clit, making her come again and again.

Mitch stopped, his shorts still on. "Sweetie, sweet Corinne, I really can't go any farther than this. Not that I don't want to, but not without hurting you. And despite how you feel right now, you're going to be plenty sore tomorrow, even with Sylvie's little nudges. You're healing faster, but it's still plenty painful, probably even more so. She's healed me, and I know exactly how painful it can get."

"Sylvie can heal people?" asked Corinne. She didn't have to ask why they were keeping that secret. A very hideous picture of an eleven-year-old girl in some sort of lab being experimented on popped into her mind and made her shiver.

"Nope, she can only accelerate healing in someone who's already doing that. Broken bones, making antibiotics more effective, that sort of thing. We have no idea how the hell it works, but we do know that it's intensely painful for the patient, and that it takes a lot of Sylvie. She and her mom go down to rock the newborns in the neonatal unit. Sylvie insists she is becoming more powerful, can hold on to the healing a bit longer, that it takes a little less out of her each time. She feels really bad about hurting the babies, but they tend to leave inten-sive care a lot faster. Apparently she can do wonders for drug-addicted babies. Sylvie's mom makes sure that both of them hold the babies, spend the same amount of time with them, so no one can be sure exactly what's happening, or who's doing what."

"Are there any more secrets you need to lay on me? You all secretly teleport, move things with your minds, or can fly?"

Mitch laughed. "We do know of some eagle, hawk, and falcon shapeshifters. They normally don't shapeshift into anything smaller, because they can very easily be taken down by predators or a kid with a BB gun." Mitch looked down, and groaned. "Shouldn't have done the talking. It's never good for Mr. Happy."

Corinne covered her eyes and groaned. "You named your penis Mr. Happy? What are you, twelve?" Mitch lunged for her, caught her in a kiss. She reached down and stroked him. "Looks like he's happy again," she said, smiling.

"What are you going to do with it now that you've caught it?" Mitch asked. Corinne grinned, and bared her teeth. Mitch recoiled and laughed at the same time. "Not anywhere near Mr. Happy. I have become somewhat attached to him."

Corinne laid back against the pillows and laughed until she snorted. "Ow, ow, ow. Painkillers before manual stimulation."

Mitch stood and padded downstairs, completely naked. He came back up with a glass of water, her pain meds, and chunks of her chocolate salted caramel bar so she didn't have to eat her meds on an empty stomach. Then he blew her mind by stroking himself in front of her, her hand cupping his balls, the taste of chocolate and caramel in her mouth, until he came. He carefully took off the sling, drew a hot bath, lifted her and gently placed her in the water. Mitch washed her hair and put on conditioner, scrubbed her back, and left her melting in there while he gave himself a shower. He dried himself off, shaved, watched her scrub herself from her face to her toes, rinsed her hair for her, drained the tub, lifted her out, gave her a small towel for her hair and a larger one for her body, and thoroughly dried her off.

Mitch brought a chair in front of the desk in the corner of the bedroom, went downstairs, and brought back up her creams and lotions, her hair brush, hairdryer, and a single ponytail holder. She sat and put on her creams and lotions while he blow-dried her hair, put it in a tight French braid, and put a ponytail holder on the end. "Where the hell did you learn how to French braid?" Corinne asked.

"Dressage. I worked as a groomsman in one of the big stables for a while. I thought about having horses, but James is gone too often and too long to help me with them."

His eyes clouded over. Corinne turned around, took his face in her hands. "Stop being angry with your brother. You both lost far too much. You need your family. I take it they are all shapeshifters too?"

"Yep. Wolf, puma, coyote, dog. Have no idea why we get along with the puma so well, but she's gone a lot."

"Stretcher," guessed Corinne. Mitch nodded, put his mouth against her neck. "You said we just now, not them," observed Corinne. He stiffened a bit. She stroked his back, then said, "Let's go to bed." Mitch gave her a Metallica T-shirt. She grinned, and he helped her slide it on. They got the sling back on, and new underwear. He led her to the bedroom, pulled back the sheets, kissed her gently, and lay her down in his bed. His arm over her hip, they both slid into sleep.

# RETURN

*J*ames came back from his fishing trip, exhausted and smelly. He cleaned the fish, and Mitch as Blackie went out to eat the fish guts, making Corinne gag. James sliced the fish into filets, put them in special packaging, and put half in the freezer and half in the refrigerator on the carport, the one that Mitch usually used for his drinks while he worked. James then literally hosed himself down with a garden hose, and sprayed Blackie off thoroughly as well. Blackie shook off, gave a little nod to James and Corinne looking out the window, and headed off into the forest.

James came in, and said, "If you don't want to see it, don't look." He stripped down to his birthday suit and made a dash for the downstairs shower. Corinne used the opportunity to notice that James was bigger in the chest, which came to a triangle. The man had obviously done quite a bit of swimming. His muscles were long and ropy, and he was a deep nut brown after all of the hiking and fishing he'd been doing. James had a scar across his back and one on his leg, and she decided to ask him about that later. Knowing the brothers, they had probably been fighting and he'd fallen off a cliff or something.

Corinne used the grabbing tool that she normally used to get items off the top shelves, picked up his clothes, and dropped them into the washer. She checked the pockets, relieved to find them empty, and that she hadn't impaled herself on a fishhook. She went outside to hose down his hiking boots. She then went back to his truck to see if there were any clothes in his gear, and found some T-shirts and shorts. She checked the pockets and used the grabber to add those to the laundry. She didn't wash the fishing vest or hat, leaving them for James to deal with when he got out of the shower. Sje started the laundry, washed up, and headed towards the kitchen for a Coke.

James came back down wearing only a blue towel, and sniffed deeply. He started humming the song "Sex and Candy." He turned suddenly, and looked at Corinne, who was just settling back onto the recliner to do more Internet marketing work for various clients. "Are you all right?" He asked. "You're not...sore? I don't mean down there..." His cheeks began turning red.

Corinne stared at James. "That's blunt, even for me, and I have ADD. We have more important things to talk about. Yes, I know your brother can turn into a wolf-dog thing, and he showed me a gray-black wolf too, this afternoon. We both prefer the wolf-dog, Blackie. And no, he wouldn't tell me what anyone else can change into directly, but he did let it slip that Stretcher is the mountain lion. Since you're brothers, I'm assuming you share the same genetics, and there is a wolf in there somewhere. Or a dog. Or both. Don't really care, kind of my first shapeshifter thing."

James stared at her as if poleaxed. "He told you..."

"No, he showed me. And, yes, we did have sex. In his bedroom, so you don't have to be worried about eating on the actual table." James turned an interesting shade of scarlet at that joke. "And no, he didn't hurt me. We haven't..." Corinne stood up, then made one finger in a circle on the other a pointer finger, and slowly brought them closer together.

James stepped forward, and grabbed her hands. "I don't need a visual, thank you."

"Will this make it weird for us? He was kind of...bleeding inside. Mitch needed a...a human bandage."

James looked Corinne in the eyes. "So, you don't consider your-self... exclusive?"

"Mitch said something to me the night of the almost-fight that didn't make sense to me before, but I think it makes sense to me now. He said that I can sleep with no one else except you."

James reached out, and touched Corinne's hair. "I think he...I think we can...I don't want to hurt my brother."

"One of the guys in college, Keifer, had two girlfriends. Everyone loved each other and they shared an apartment, so nobody gave a rat's ass except for the Pearl People."

"Pearl People?" James looked confused. Corinne pretended to finger pearls around her neck. "Oh. They wear pearls on Sundays, think they should tell everyone else how to live their lives?"

Corinne nodded. "My mother is exactly like that, but the weird thing is she didn't really care about what I did. She cared about how she looked."

"No one should ignore you," said James, touching her hair again. "I have no idea how anyone managed to do that."

"I don't either," said Corinne, with an impish smile. "I'm awesome. If they can't figure that out, they can jump in a frozen lake and die slowly of hypothermia."

James let out a laugh. "Interesting visual," he said.

The back door opened, and James whirled to look at his brother, a man again, wearing worn jean shorts. "Will the two of you have sex already?" asked Mitch. "You can get your own girl if you want, but you won't find anyone like Corinne. Besides, I can smell that you like her from here."

"Eww. Go back outside, or take a damn shower. Your brother and I are busy." Corinne stepped forward, touched James' hand to get his attention, then gave up and walked around to face him. She went up on her tiptoes, grabbed his face in her hands, and kissed him. James put one arm around her good side, carefully braced her arm with the other.

"I'll just get some..." said Mitch. He went out the back door, shut it, and soon a black dog streaked across the yard in front of the back window.

James let her go, looked down into her eyes. "You don't mind sharing us?" he asked, gently.

"You're the ones that are going to have to share me. And, as I just said, I am extraordinary."

James smiled wider and wider, then bent down, carefully took her face in his hands, his fingers in her hair, and kissed her deeply. "You are extraordinary," he said.

"I have ADD, I curse like a sailor, and I throw pencils when I'm angry. And I suck at being injured."

James kissed away her recitation of her flaws. "Magnificent."

Somehow, the towel ended up on the floor. James walked behind Corinne on their way up the stairs, one hand on her hip to prevent her from falling. "Must get a railing," said James, as they moved up the stairs as quickly as Corinne's arm would allow.

"Later," said Corinne, dragging James into his room. This one had shelves full of rocks, dried flowers, the requisite county map, a highly detailed trail map, the same platform bed in black as his brother and Stretcher. James rushed forward to pile up the pillows. Corinne laughed. "I'm not a porcelain doll."

"You're right," said James. He got a condom box out of the left-hand nightstand drawer, threw it onto the dresser. He carefully helped her take off the sling, then took her shirt off on the non-injured side first. He got her out of her shorts and panties, and then had her stand facing the dresser, completely nude. He stroked her from her head all the way down to her toes and back on each side, then in front. He sucked each breast, nibbling just a bit, walking the line between pleasure and pain. She came, hard, and he smiled. He carefully put the sling back on her, bent her over the dresser.

He tore the condom wrapper off with his teeth and rolled it on, put her hand up on the wall, his hand on top. He slid into her, just inside, and reached around and used his fingers to drive her insane. He pressed, licked his fingers, and teased her until she came again. He slid in, a little bit at a time, making sure she could take all of him. When he was all the way in, he put the hand back onto her hand, and his other around her waist to pull her tight. He went in and out very slowly at first, teasing her, then went faster and faster.

James was always careful, holding her back from the wall so she wouldn't bang her shoulder. James touched her again, and made her come so hard that she saw stars. He came with her, and stood there, gasping. He carefully drew himself out of her, holding onto the condom. She lay her good shoulder against the wall, and gasped as he went into the bathroom, came back with a wet washcloth. He cleaned them both up, threw the washcloth in the dirty clothes hamper, and led her to the bed. They both lay there, trying to breathe.

Corinne said, "You're going to have to be on a schedule, and I'm going to need some time to recover. I can't keep jostling this damn shoulder. We're going to have to work around you first, because you're the one that's gone all the time."

James looked into her eyes, stroked her hair. "Corinne, you are the most beautiful woman I've ever seen. Your eyes light up when you laugh, you're one of the hardest workers I've ever seen, and you just don't give up. I saw you at your most broken, and you didn't give up anything. You were a bloody mess, still ready to do whatever you need to do. That is absolutely extraordinary. Whatever schedule you make, I'll make do. You're worth it. If my brother and I get a woman as extraordinary as you, if we have you in our lives, we will do whatever it takes to make it work for you." Corinne looked over at James, then laughed. "What?" he asked.

"It's about time someone looked at me the way the two of you do. Your whole face lights up. It's like...like I'm the best candy in the candy store, the bike you've always wanted, the waterfall you find after three hours of hiking. You make me feel desired."

"Whoever didn't do that is an idiot who can't add two and two to make four. This is your home now, baby."

Corinne sat up in bed, startling James. "What about Miz Raynelle? She needs that rent money."

James laughed and guided her back down. "Seems to me you've got a friend at the coffee shop who needs a low-rent place to live. Why don't you talk to her? And, we will do anything around the house that your former landlord needs. She treated you damn well when you arrived, and we don't forget favors around here."

Corinne nodded, then lay back against James. "We'll do that, then."

James smiled at her and kissed her forehead. "Let's try turning that beautiful brain off for awhile. I've just been standing in ice-cold creeks listening to fat men who liked to tell stories. A little peace and quiet would be nice, preferably without the whir of the wheels in your brain turning."

"What kind of stories did the fat men like to talk about?"

"Football in high school, meeting their wives, work and friendship, kids and barbecues. They are both sales managers in different parts of the state, meet once a year to drink beer and tell tall tales." James gently stroked her hair.

Corinne said, "It's already been forever since I saw Kandace and Tania. Video calls are not the same thing."

"Well then. Let's get your loans paid off so you can go visit them." Both James and Mitch had seen the chart Corinne pulled up when she made a payment. Corinne didn't owe anything from college, but she had secretly taken out loans that she had called "scholarships" for both of her friends to help defray the enormous costs of college all the way through to graduate school. Corinne had a repayment plan, and made significant dents in it as she took on more clients and charged more money. "It was a really good thing you did for your friends."

"Even renting ebooks costs money. But, it's worth it to see them both doing things that they want to do. Tania is overseas, in Asia, and Kandace found a cabin where she went to 'get clear with herself.' I'm not entirely sure where she is; she won't tell us. I think it's in the Ozarks, probably in Arkansas, but she may be somewhere else, like the Appalachians. She says we can't visit her until she pays off her own spreadsheet of loans."

"You women are damn serious about your debts." James kissed her hair.

"Can't move forward in life without them being paid off."

James stroked her cheek. "Let's get you some new clients. Later. There's a lot we haven't done yet." He kissed her, barely a brush of his lips.

"You're so tired, you're going to fall asleep in my hair." She held him and stroked his back until he slid under.

# MOVING DAY

*I*t took only one truckload to get the rest of Corinne's clothes and things. James and Mitch packed up the truck while Corinne dusted and mopped, making the place ready for Dana. James and Mitch then worked their way down Corinne's punch list for Miz Raynelle's home. They replaced the back porch stairs, kitchen backsplash, and broken tiles in the downstairs bathroom, and hired a roofer to replace the thing rather than do a patch job.

Corinne and Miz Raynelle sat out on the big white porch in Adirondack chairs sipping fresh-squeezed lemonade and eating peanut butter cookies while half-naked men and one woman replaced the roof and Mitch helped Dana bring her stuff into her new apartment. Miz Raynelle said, "The view is very nice today, isn't it?" They both laughed. The sound of banging led to a curse. James stuck his head over the side of the roof and said, "Sorry, Miz Raynelle."

Miz Raynelle laughed. "Oh, my virgin ears!" Corinne laughed too, and sipped more lemonade.

Dana came down, and Mitch took off his shirt and shimmied up the ladder. "Thanks so much, Corinne, for telling me about this place. I was getting damn sick of my brother." She accepted the glass of lemonade Miz Raynelle poured, and said, "Sorry, Miz Raynelle."

"If my brother was doing what your brother was, I would have a thing or two to say about it myself. I am sorry he's so ill." Dana's brother was known around town as Rooney the Loonie. He refused to take any medication for his manic depression, except alcohol and whatever pills he could cadge from somebody. He supposedly worked at the diner as a dishwasher; Dana's father had him on the payroll. But, he rarely showed up for work. When he did, he cursed loudly enough to be heard in the dining room, broke dishes, and stole tips if he could.

"How are you doing with the Internet marketing class?" Corinne asked.

Dana winced. "It's a pain in the ass—in the behind, sorry, Miz Raynelle—but when I get it right, it's like a party."

Miz Raynelle smiled softly. "I always knew you were better than just waiting tables, not that there's anything wrong with that, but your brain is strong and fast. I can see you working with your mind instead of your hands. You're gonna move away when you're done with all your schooling?"

Dana shook her head. "I've got choices now. Corinne says I can take a lot of busywork off her hands. She'd like more time to work directly with clients, signing up new ones, and do some real complicated websites for 'em. I can use my photography, too. I've gone hiking up in the mountains on my days off, taking pictures of the flowers, deer, and such. Corinne says I can sell these pictures online as stock pictures, make a few dollars per picture."

Corinne nodded. "You can only make tips in the diner while you're there, but you can make money off your photos all day, every day, selling them online. You can also go to festivals and contests, take pictures and make money off that. City councils or committees might pay good money for those pictures."

"Oh, they've got all sorts of festivals and trade shows round here, and stuff like Cinco de Mayo and fishing contests, anglers gettin' that steelhead and trout. Someone might pay you to take pictures of their winning fish," said Miz Raynelle.

"I need to earn enough to buy one of Mitch's bikes, then I can go all over the county seeing what's what. But I tell you what, I better be earning more than tip money. I won't drive all over these mountains for free," Dana proclaimed, then took a peanut butter cookie.

"Wouldn't expect you to. Get yourself an online portfolio and build yourself a website with that all ready to go," counseled Corinne. "You're already doing that with your coding. Make it simple, and I'll show you how to hook up with an online retailer in order to sell your stuff."

"Those API's are a pain in the ass. Sorry, Miz Raynelle." Dana blushed.

"PIs, private investigators?" asked Miz Raynelle.

Dana shook her head."No. APIs are little pieces of code that let you put stuff from other websites into your website, like a clock or the weather or something. They're kind of cool, but a pain in the a—butt to get to work right."

When she was able to talk over pounding on the roof, Miz Raynelle said, "That all sounds like too much for me." She sipped her lemonade, looked up, and smiled a little smile. "Anybody like what you see?" she asked, looking upward.

"You are so bad," said Dana, with a laugh. Corinne laughed too.

"I'm old, not dead," said Miz Raynelle. They all laughed even harder.

Mitch and James came down from the roof, covered with sweat. They went to the garden hose, drank the water, and then sprayed themselves all over. They shook themselves all over like dogs, making Corinne double over with laughter, her ribs finally healed. Miz Raynelle and Dana were too polite to ask what she was laughing about. "I think it's time to take these men home," said Corinne. "We were up at dawn, didn't have our usual big breakfast. They'll probably want more barbecue at the barbecue place so they don't have to cook."

Corinne stood up and said, "Ma'am, you call us every six months, earlier if you want, to come down and do whatever you need on your house. And I don't want to hear anyone talking back," she said mock-glaring at Miz Raynelle. "Thank you for the lemonade and cookies, but I've got two uncouth males to feed." She looked up.

"Mabel is still up there." Mabel was the woman from the roofing company Corinne had seen in the hardware store months ago. The woman moved on the roof with grace and could use a nail gun like a military shooter. She was up on the roof with her oldest, Ashe, a fine-looking young man in jeans with a ripped body. Corinne only had eyes for her men.

Miz Raynelle said, "Them men sure are easy on the eyes."

"That they are," said Corinne. She had to work hard not to put all her lascivious thoughts into her voice. "See you fine ladies later." She hopped off the porch, grinned, and sauntered toward the truck.

"Do you think she's doing them both?" asked Miz Raynelle. Dana let out a startled bark of laughter. Corinne, on her way to the truck, put her hand over her mouth. Her shoulders shook with laughter.

~

James dialed ahead while Mitch drove. "You do realize you are going to have to hose down the inside of this truck with disinfectant after all the time you spent on the roof?" asked Corinne.

"This here is a working man's truck," said Mitch. "Expect there to be sweat, spilled beer, and the occasional loose French fries on the floorboards."

"Eww," said Corinne. "And I expect you to have this thing detailed before I get back in it."

James grinned as he ordered several slabs of pork ribs, biscuits, honey and butter, two orders of corn on the cob, potato salad, and drinks to go using his cell phone. "We could go in, but I even offend myself at this point."

"Roll down the windows. You're offending the hell out of me." Mitch flipped her off, and James rolled down the windows. Sissy from the barbecue place ran out with their huge order, and Corinne took it and put it on the back seat.

Mitch drove as if the truck bed was on fire, making Corinne grab onto the "oh god" bar. "Slow down, or I'm going to punch you with my good hand," said Corinne, white-lipped. "The sling is not completely off yet, and this hurts like hell."

James looked back at her, and said, in a growly voice, "Slow down, Mitch. You're hurting our woman."

Mitch looked in the rearview mirror, saw Corinne's clenched jaw, and said, "I apologize, baby." He slowed down, but still made record time up the mountain.

Mitch grabbed the food and took it inside, while James came around the car, opened the door, and helped Corinne out of the king cab-sized truck. "I don't know what got into Mitch. Don't worry, I'll beat him up later. Right now, let's get you inside, and sit you down in your recliner with some ice. I'll bring you some pills, and get you a tray so you can eat your lunch." James opened up the carport door and led her inside. He helped her sit, put out the tray, brought over an ice pack from the freezer, her medication, and a glass of water, and ran upstairs for a quick shower.

Both Mitch and James were downstairs in less than seven minutes from cleaning themselves up. Mitch passed out the food, and began devouring it as if the food was going to get up and run away from him. James carefully sliced the ribs, separating them so Corinne could eat them. He brought her several napkins and a fork, and her sides. He left his brother alone at the table, and James sat down next to Corinne on the couch with his own tray. He remembered the drinks, got up, and brought them over. He pulled up their streaming movie service, and went to their Watch Later list. "Ex-Mossad hitwoman on the run, an alien family from Alpha Centauri living in the suburbs, three family women that defeat drug dealers in their spare time, and something with a lot of half-naked people on the beach."

"Alpha Centauri," said Corinne. "Then the ex-Mossad thing. Love that one."

"Hey!" said Mitch. "One, why aren't you sitting here with me at the table? I no longer stink. Two, isn't it a good thing to have half-naked people at the beach?"

"Half-naked people at the beach, number three," said Corinne.

"I've got no problem with that." James clicked on the correct show, snagged a rib, and started chewing on it.

"Hey!" Mitch near-bellowed. "Why are you guys over there and I'm over here?"

"One, I'm too damn busy eating to sit around talking. Two, you drove like Mario Andretti and banged my shoulder around. Three, your brother gave me drugs. I take drugs over the kitchen table." Corinne finished her potato salad, wondering where it had all gone.

Mitch stood up, put the plate with the bones on the floor, stripped down, turned himself into a dog, and started gnawing on the bones under the kitchen table. Corinne grinned, and said, "So that's why you guys never have bones or table scraps, let alone leftovers! If you guys had crops, you would suck at composting."

James let out a surprised belly laugh. "We don't grow crops because Mitch is too damn lazy, I'm gone all the time, and Rachael sends Stretcher over with a produce basket twice a week. She used to leave it under cover of darkness, but I've asked Stretcher to come in and relax with us, rather than have to run around in the dark. It's been nice to come out of the familial closet, so to speak."

"Have you talked to Gunny?" asked Corinne.

"Not today," said James. Satisfied, Corinne finished her meal while watching the aliens try to figure out what school was and why their offspring would have to attend. Corinne brought her and James' bones over to the table, and slid them underneath. Mitch-as-Blackie nuzzled her hand and licked her fingers. Corinne washed the honey from the biscuits off her hands, cleaned up the detritus from the meal, and sat back down to cuddle with James. Blackie became Mitch and put shorts on just in time for the half-naked beach people movie, put shorts on, and rubbed Corinne's feet in apology.

Corinne waited until James had gone to the kitchen to get a soda and pop some popcorn. Then, she reached over and grabbed Mitch's hand. "You were twelve years old when your parents died, and that's pretty much where your emotional growth ended. When you get angry, you hurt yourself and the people around you. News flash, Mitch. You're not twelve years old anymore. You're twenty-five. If you ever act that way to me again like you did today, bouncing me around like a ping-pong ball when you know that my shoulder still hurts, we are going to break up hard. That means looking at me every day, with your brother. And you can't do a twelve-year-old thing like make a smirk or a cute face or a halfhearted apology and get me back. You will grow the hell up right now, if we are going to have a relationship."

Mitch looked in those beautiful eyes of hers, and nodded once. He knew when a woman laid down the law. That was it, if you wanted a relationship.

# DELIVERY

*R*achael came down herself for the next delivery during daylight hours. She knocked on the carport door, and Corinne let her in. Corinne reached for the hefty basket Rachael carried, but Rachael waved her off. "Well, at least it smells better around here. Less like a wet dog." Rachael marched over to the kitchen, put the giant basket on the counter, pulled out a cutting board and both a paring and butcher knife, and started pulling things out of the basket. "Sit a spell. I do apologize, because I know you have someone working for you, and that's even more work than you started out with."

Corinne snorted out a laugh. "Dana literally records everything she does, but I'm able to speed it up and focus on the important parts. But, sometimes I have quite a bit of video to sort through. She hasn't made any fundamental mistakes yet. She understands color, balance, and light, things that are extremely hard to teach. She even created a marketing video for me, really just bits and pieces with some art and with quotes moving around the screen. Twenty-five seconds of really good art, though."

Rachael rinsed a tomato, and began dicing it with quick, firm strokes. "Dana has always been a really bright young woman. I teach physical education at two high schools, and coach the field hockey, volleyball, and cross-country skiing teams. Creates a lot more work and driving, and we still have the farm. Dana took field hockey for two years. She has a brother, like a millstone around the family neck because he won't take his damn meds." Rachael took out a second tomato, rinsed it, and diced it just as quickly as the first. "Do you have any siblings, Corinne?"

"My brother was almost nine years older. I was kind of a surprise, and an unwanted one at that. Dad had the son who would follow in his academic footsteps, and he did. Lane's got some fellowship in Japan, I think. We haven't communicated in over a decade. My mother cashed out of her law practice, works as a professor's wife, putting on these really lavish parties and lots of not being home; mostly sitting on boards. She gardens. Well, she did, now she just tells the gardener what she wants done. Anyway, the only time my parents noticed me was to quiz me about something. My dad is a physics professor, so I was learning about quantum theory before I could do my multiplication tables. I grew up in a holler just outside the tiny university town when I was little because it was so much cheaper than university housing, until he scored the professor house near campus. Being smart didn't really work as an asset when my father was a misogynist. He slept with the coeds and plagiarized from everyone in order to get published. But, he wrote really excellent letters of recommendation to prestigious universities and got grants for students, so he got away with it. I decided to go with the free ride, had my parents pay my way through my master's degrees. Online marketing and information science, plus a lot of English courses. Copywriting."

Rachael switched from tomatoes to carrots. She put the tomatoes in a little plastic dish, and put a lid on it. "The secret is olive oil in the dish. It keeps the plastic from turning colors." The carrots she rinsed and peeled were white, the standard orange, and purple. "We grow heirloom vegetables. We live and die by the land. Built a vertical farm in an unused building, so we can grow things year-round now. Make a lot of money selling produce to restaurants." She finished peeling a white carrot and started on an orange one. "Your upbringing sounds very cold, and somewhat horrible. You didn't get any fathering. I assume you didn't get any mothering either?"

"Nope. Housekeepers, mostly. No one actually was called a nanny, but they knew what they were supposed to do. Mom just...the affairs didn't seem to bother her. Kind of a heart of ice."

"That's where you get your hardness from, I reckon. Not knocking it, just noticing. It makes you strong enough for my boys. Stretcher says you chose them both? She has the nose to smell that sort of thing."

Corinne nodded, and shrugged. "I found out in college that how many people you love has nothing to do with the quality of your love, as long as everyone is honest about it. The guy I knew in college, Keifer. Last I heard the two he was with in college are still with him. Not sisters or anything, either. Said he just happened to fall in love with two people at the same time, and didn't understand why he would have to choose."

"That's a mature point of view." Rachael put the carrot strips into another plastic container. She pulled out red, green, and orange bell peppers and started cutting them into strips after washing them in the sink. "Mitch is not as mature as he should be. Is he giving you trouble?"

"Yes, until I put a stop to it. I told him his parents may have died when he was twelve, and that he stopped growing emotionally at that point, but I wouldn't put up with his twelve-year-old behavior when he's twenty-five. He gets angry and hurts people like a child, and I will not tolerate it. He physically hurt me by driving like a maniac home in a snit, and I told him that will never happen again unless he wants us to break up real hard."

"I suspect he was hangry. Have you noticed the boys will go through five meals a day, sometimes six? Full meals? Shifters need more food, because it takes energy to shift. We have to shift, or we eventually go insane. We also have to shift back because we simply cannot maintain the animal until we get very old. Then, some of us choose to live out the rest of our lives that way rather than dealing with dementia or Alzheimer's. They go wolf or dog or hawk, whatever they are, and stay that way."

"James told me that most shifters choose predators so that they don't get eaten or killed by bigger animals in their shapeshifting forms. If I may ask, what do you turn into?"

"Coyote, or a wolf. I got myself into an otter once, but I was a really big otter, and looked ridiculous. I did it when I was a kid, thinking otters were cute. Coons are big, and I was one of them once when I needed to get up a tree. I have no idea why I was able to turn into a coon while no one else in my family seems to be able to do it." Rachael finished the bell peppers, put them in their plastic container. She rinsed a cucumber, then sliced it into rounds.

"Are you able to shift as babies?"

Rachael laughed. "I've heard of shifters shifting as early as three or four, but most don't start until they are between six and seven years old. No, that would be a right mess." She finished with the first cucumber, selected a second one.

"What happens if a shifter mates with a non-shifter, can the baby still shift?"

"You mean, is shifting dominant or recessive? Well, it seems to be dominant. Three out of four children that are born to a shifter and a non-shifter parent tend to become shifters. You would think that, because it is a dominant trait, there wouldn't be so few of us. But, hunting, environmental degradation, and the need for secrecy keep our families small, and we hold the secret dear. I really don't feel like having this done to me on some metal table," Rachael said, gesturing with the paring knife.

"Or being forced to work for the government, or being tested as to what shifters can and can't turn into, the list goes on and on. Yeah, I've got the picture. Whatever happens, I will not expose you, any of you." Corinne sighed. "I don't even know what James turns into. He says he only shifts alone, out in the forest. He says that's why being a guide is so vital to him, why it's so important that he keeps his job no matter what. And, I guess, the search and rescue." Corinne sighed and looked up at Rachael. "I assume Mitch heard me crashing around up there and went to investigate."

"We all heard the howl. James was already on the mountain checking a trail for deadfall, so he triangulated from the howls where his brother was. He called down to us and we made everything ready. Putting together a stretcher out of nothing wasn't easy. We've gone ahead and ordered a real stretcher and a bunch of medical supplies in case something like that ever happens again. Spirit willing, it won't. But, you never know, so we prepare, prepare, and prepare some more."

"I take it you have rules. What do I need to know?"

Rachael looked at Corinne through narrowed eyes, apparently liked what she saw, then nodded once. "First, keep the secret at all costs, even at the cost of your life, your spouse, your children. Second, no shifter ever hunts another except for when one of us commits a heinous crime such as exposing us or harming a child. We can smell each other, even as humans. Pheromones. Third, no shifter community can interfere with any other shifter community. They are all completely self-supporting, and usually rather isolated. We've scattered ourselves all over the globe, to be sure that at least some of us survive. Last, we must come to the aid of other shifter communities to protect the secret, or ensure their survival. We can't afford to lose communities. They're kind of like organs in the human body. You can only lose so many of them before you die. Oh, and we don't hunt humans. Cannibals get destroyed. We've only had one instance like that in modern times, and there was an accident on an island. We don't like riding on boats or planes for that reason. Getting stranded is not good for us."

"I will follow all of the rules."

"There is one more thing, followed even more now than before. People get tattoos of their spouse's animals on their shoulders, or another place that can easily be covered by clothing. There is a special symbol we work along the edges, and it marks you as someone who knows and keeps our secret. It's also a tad dangerous, because everyone will know if you break any of our rules."

Corinne shrugged. "My shoulder hurts anyway, and I have some pretty good drugs left over. I can get it done today, or as soon as I figure out what the hell James turns himself into."

"A gray and black wolf. He is very strong and can move at speeds that even Gunny has trouble keeping up with. It broke our hearts when they left, but they had to. They had to become their own men, disentangle themselves from the emotional trauma. Looking at us every day just brought it all back." Rachael took out flour, sugar, and cinnamon. "We can make carrot cake muffins and banana nut bread." Rachael pointed at the bananas in a bowl on the table. She pulled out a bag of shelled, halved pecans from the cupboard.

Corinne grabbed the bananas and handed them to Rachael. "I can't imagine having to let them go in order for them to heal. That took courage beyond anything I've ever seen before."

Rachael put the bananas down, turned, and looked Corinne in the eyes. "First, you've shown amazing courage yourself, fighting back against an attacker, getting away, and making it down the mountain, badly injured. Second, you brought our boys back to us. Mitch is still a mess, and may be for months yet. You gave him the kickboxing gym to work out his feelings. I wish I had thought of that. Third, I've never seen those boys so happy, fired up, willing to do whatever it is they need to do. Stretcher says they have actual conversations with her without trying to bite her head off. Whatever the hell you did, we owe you. If you need anything from any of us, a helping hand, money, a car, a toothbrush at four in the morning, you call us first. It's our job to take care of our family, and no matter what happens between you and our boys, you are now family."

Corinne was startled to feel Rachael's arms around her waist instead of her shoulders so she wouldn't hurt the arm. Corinne reached up, hugged her back, and was startled to find tears streaming down her face.

Rachael let her go, reached up to wipe away Corinne's tears, and kissed her forehead. "Now, the muffins. Would you like to measure out the flour?"

Corinne laughed, wiped her eyes, went into the kitchen, washed her hands, pulled out a drawer, and found the measuring cup. "Ready." And, she was.

# DEEP WATERS

*J*ames padded into the kitchen barefoot, wearing gray shorts and a blue sleeveless shirt, talking on his cell phone using an ear bud and throat mic. Rachael had the chicken breast on the cutting board, dripping juices. She sliced it into thin slices. "No, she's not a toy we play with. She's a person. Not a prize. And what the hell is this any of your business anyway?" He stepped past both Rachael and Corinne, kissing each woman on the cheek from behind as he went by. He stopped in front of the refrigerator, opened it, grabbed a cola, closed it, and popped the top. "No, we don't. Ugh! Would you really want to see your brother naked?"

Corinne opened the door to the oven, grabbed a toothpick out of the toothpick holder, and inserted it into a muffin, then one on another tray. Both times the toothpicks came out clean, so she put on an oven mitt and pulled the trays out one at a time. She put them on the stove burners, then shut the oven door. James reached below her into a thin cabinet, the one that held the muffin trays, baking sheets, and other baking supplies. He pulled out two wire racks, put his soda down, flipped the feet up on the racks, put them on top of the stove above the burners, grabbed his soda, kissed Corinne's cheek, and stepped out of the kitchen. "Yes, she can swim. Because she's talked about a housekeeper who signed her up for swim lessons, doofus. Well, I don't know. She's still recovering from the..."

Corinne walked past Rachael, tapped James' shoulder, and made a swimming motion with her good arm. James nodded. "Well, we do have those water skiing life vests. We can put her in it, tie up her arm so it doesn't move with those rubber bands you used to work out. No, we won't bring any damn potato salad. Who do you think is going to make it?" Corinne walked back and used a butter knife to pop the muffins out. Corinne put the muffins on the cooling racks, sprayed cooking oil spray onto both pans, then used a scoop to fill each one up with the correct batter, half carrot, half banana nut. She slid each pan into the oven, then shut it.

"No, dumbass, I'm going to spend the next four days on trails, all over to hell and back. Mitch has two bikes he's got to knock out in a row. He's been working until close to midnight each night to get them done." James snorted into the phone. "Did you forget she has full use of only one arm?" He dropped his soda off at the table, saw the bowl of salad, walked to the fridge, took the salad dressings out of the refrigerator with one hand, and reached over Corinne's head to take out the salad bowls then brought them over to the table.

Rachael took the potatoes out of the oven that she had washed, stabbed with forks, and rolled in salt, then foil. She gently unwrapped them, sliced them open, and pressed the ends together to make them fluff out. "Doritos, two-liters, or both. Make up your damn mind." James went back for plates, and Corinne took out the cream cheese, butter, and cream for the frosting out of the refrigerator. She took out the small canister of confectioners' sugar, a bowl, and measuring cups and spoons. Rachael switched with her, and Corinne began dressing the salad with pecans, cranberries, and the chicken. Corinne swung behind Rachael, took out bacon bits from the refrigerator, shut the door, and went back over to dump them on the salad.

"Okay, both it is. No, I have no idea if Mitch will come or not. He's still in a pissy mood. Corinne apparently pulled his chain, because he's been behaving a lot better. Neither one of them will tell me what she said to calm him the hell down." Rachael added almond extract to the ingredients, took out the mixer, mixed the frosting, and began frosting the muffins. She grinned at Corinne, and Corinne grinned back. Corinne found the wooden fork and spoon used to toss the salad, and stuck them in the salad bowl without doing any of the tossing. James came over, tossed the salad, and put it on the table in the middle.

James came back to the kitchen for cloth napkins. "No, she doesn't stay here twenty-four hours a day. When I'm here, she'll ask to go to the diner, coffee shop, or barbecue place, maybe the mall, and I'll ask her whether or not she wants me to call Dana. She says 'Yes, please,' and I dropped them both off to do whatever the hell it is they do. Sometimes Dana has a shift at the diner, or she talks way too much business when Corinne is trying to relax." James grabbed forks, then walked to the table and put napkins under the forks. "No, I don't know what the hell she does at the mall. I do whatever the hell I've got going on, then come back."

Corinne snorted, went over to James, pulled the earphone out of his ear, and talked into it. "Stretcher, there's this set of nesting weights that I really want. I can't get it yet. Because, duh. No, not that brand. The other one. I also can't try on exercise gear unless it's an XL, because I can't get my arm in the hole otherwise. Two sounds good. Gotta go, Rachael cooked. Yeah, I guess we have enough, if you're really close. If not, we'll have it gone before you even..." There was a knock at the door, and Corinne pulled the earbud out of her ear and handed it back. James snorted, took the earbud back, cut off the call, and opened the back door.

Stretcher wore black shades with dark red lenses, a black Nike workout shirt, and black shorts with a silver racing stripe down each side. In keeping with the Nike theme, her shoes were Nike gel-soled running shoes, vented for summer. Her black hair was freshly buzzed. She looked like a commercial, except for the jagged scar right next to her hairline on the left side.

Rachael took one look at Stretcher, and said, "Wash up."

"Hello to you, too." Stretcher snorted. She waved at Corinne, gave

James a nod, kicked off her shoes in the doorway, and race-walked over to the bathroom.

"Did you really just call Stretcher a dumbass?" asked Corinne.

"Every day in every way," said James, with a grin.

Corinne punched his shoulder. "And what the hell is it with you people and potato salad? I think you're potato salad addicts." She crossed over to the refrigerator, took out a block of cheddar cheese. James crossed over, grabbed a bowl and a shredder, unwrapped the cheese, and shredded cheese directly into the bowl. Corinne patted his cheek, then took out the sour cream and grabbed what was left of the bacon bits. She put them on the table, then went back for a collection of sodas that she put in the middle of the table.

Stretcher came out of the bathroom, crossed back over from whence she came, stuck her head out of the door, and whistled so loudly that Corinne dropped the sour cream onto the table. "Damn, woman!" Corinne complained to Stretcher. "You ever wake the dead with that whistle?"

"Not lately." Stretcher surveyed the table, then went over to the kitchen and took out a spoon for the sour cream.

They all stood behind their chairs at the table, not bothering to wait for Mitch. It would take him at least five minutes to scrub his hands at the outside sink. They all held their hands at their shoulders, palms out, and Rachael sang, "Spirit move us, guide us, direct us to protect ourselves and serve others, and to be at the service of life."

"Spirit move us," said James and Stretcher. After a beat, Corinne said it too. They all sat down, and passed around the salad, potatoes, and salad dressings. Rachael put the remaining salad and a potato on a plate for Mitch.

Mitch came in, narrowed his eyes and he saw that everyone was eating, stood behind his chair, held his hands up, and said, "Spirit move us." He sat down, and gruffly said, "Thank you for bringing your bounty, Rachael, and for staying to help prepare it."

"It's nice not to have to sneak out at five in the morning to bring it over," said Stretcher. "That was getting old."

"I'm sorry that it took so long for us to come to terms with the family," said James, glaring at his brother. James put butter, sour cream and bacon bits on his baked potato. He passed the Caesar dressing to Corinne, who smiled at him.

Mitch looked over at Corinne, and decided not to actively piss her off. "We agreed to disagree," he said, putting butter on his potato.

"And the sparring continues," said Stretcher.

"James is right, you are a dumbass," said Corinne to Stretcher. "He made an adult statement which accurately reflects how he feels. Don't go stirring the pot."

Mitch grinned, surprised that Corinne had stood up for him. "It is accurate," he said, tilting his head. He speared himself some salad.

Rachael smiled indulgently at him. "Accurate, and in spoken in a normal tone of voice. Progress, not perfection. But one hell of a lot of progress." Mitch grinned back.

"Hey!" said James. "Mitch suddenly started acting like an adult, which I've done longer than he has, and he gets all the love?" James pretended to be deeply wounded.

Stretcher laughed. "Did someone get his little feelings hurt?" She stole both a banana nut and a carrot cake muffin.

James flipped her off. "You always were an annoying sister."

Stretcher grimaced at him, but her eyes were dancing. "Mitch, we've been invited to a cookout at the farm at the end of the week. You can come or not, but it's going to be by the lake. I heard a rumor that we are going to be able to get Corinne to actually swim."

"That's easy," said Mitch, waving his fork around. "We can get some of those life jackets we use for water skiing, and tie up her arm to where she can't move it. Can't use bungee cords, too much give."

"James suggested using those rubber straps we use to exercise with," said Corinne. "We can probably buy more of them when we go shopping at two."

"James is going shopping at two?" asked Mitch, laughing.

Stretcher snorted. "No, he's dropping us off. I can't put Corinne on the back of my bike, and if there was an accident all three of you would flay me alive."

"Flaying takes too long, and would be rather messy," James pointed out. "Besides, I need to install more shelves, and pick up a better dresser. The one in there is too small and falling apart." He pointed toward Corinne's room with his knife.

"Sleep by yourself?" Stretcher asked Corinne, completely unself-consciously.

"At least one night a week, or whenever I'm really pissed off," said Corinne. Both Mitch and James spewed their sodas. Rachael grinned, and Stretcher coughed. "I need my alone time, or I become the wicked witch no one wants to be around."

James cleaned up the soda with his napkin, and so did Mitch. "That's very private information," said James.

Mitch pointed his knife at Stretcher. "You keep your feline mouth shut about this," he said, using his knife to point to himself and James. "No one needs to know about that part of our lives except us."

Rachael smiled sweetly at Stretcher. "You will respect the family and its privacy, won't you?" she said, her voice like honey, with the faint ribbon of steel lying underneath.

Stretcher was about to stir the pot some more until she parsed Rachael's tone. She looked over at Rachael, and bowed her head. "Of course."

"So, which weight set should I get?" asked Corinne. James and Mitch sparred a bit over which nested set was best. Stretcher weighed in, Rachael gave her own opinion, then everyone nodded. Corinne grinned, and attacked her salad.

# SWIM

The lake was halfway on the family's property. It was deep, nearly thirty feet at one end, and a glassy blue. There were two docks on their property, one for those who wanted to go out to the middle of the lake and put their lines in the water, and one farther down for those who were into the canoes, rowboats, and other water sports. There was one canoe on the dock and a rowboat tied to it on the left, both watercraft dark blue with orange reflective paint on the top. The lake curved around until one couldn't see in it anymore, hidden by a jutting rock on one side, trees on the other. There were houses dotting the lake on the far side.

"This lake was carved out by a really big rock, or so everyone seems to think," said James, sipping on his beer, his feet in the water. "Gouged a great big hole, and got itself broken up by wind and rain over the years. Geologists say they found pieces of it, and that it was a big mother while it was intact, thousands of years ago."

Stretcher rode a jet ski and Mitch flew behind her on water skis in the middle of the lake so the waves didn't bother those fishing off one of the docks that dotted the lakeshore or the banks. The noise did, and those fishing shook their fists at Stretcher, who laughed and went around the bend out of sight.

Corinne sipped on her strawberry lemonade, her feet in the water. The life vest hurt when they first got it on, but now her arm felt really good, tied tight so it couldn't move around by two rubber bands, a red and an orange one. "This is a fantastic lake. The property your family owns must be expensive as hell." She took another sip, enjoying the ice-cold taste on her tongue.

"Wasn't when they got it nearly a century ago. And the family is not what you think. It's more a collection of people with very hard heads. There are not that many large predators in these mountains after Teddy Roosevelt went after them." He shook his head. "The man considered himself an environmentalist, but made plenty of mistakes. He just didn't have the right information at the time." James refocused back on the story about the family. "Most of them could transform into other animals and, therefore not get eaten by something. It gave us more of a range, a repertoire if you will."

"I haven't seen any of your animals. Figure you'll show me if you ever want to do that."

James gusted out a sigh. "It's not what you think. I'm not ashamed of it. And I do have a pretty good repertoire, but I'm a big guy. A coyote is a little too small for me. What most people don't know, not even Rachael, is that Stretcher taught me how to turn into a puma."

"Wait," said Corinne. "I thought you specialized, canine, feline, bird." She didn't spill Rachael's secret that she could turn into an otter and a coon.

"I'm the only one that I know of that can do this," said James. "And I don't plan on telling the others. It was a stupid experiment to try, because I could have hurt myself or someone else."

Corinne nodded. James reached out, took Corinne's hand. "I know that you are itching to train, so you can fight back if Malcolm shows back up. I also know that you know that if you injure yourself, you're going to put your healing back, and have to get well all over again."

Corinne cut her eyes at him. "If he ever comes back, you'll be able to pick him out of the lineup. He'll be the one without a face. And, I know you're leading up to telling me that you and Mitch can protect me. But I'm not a helpless little woman. I defended myself then, and I will again. In fact, Stretcher's been teaching me knife skills, with my good hand. Throwing, attacking, defending. When she took me shopping, we ordered some pretty good blades, ones small enough for me to hide."

James looked Corinne up and down. She had on a hot pink bikini and matching bikini bottom with pink lace on the sides under her bright blue and yellow swim vest. "You don't have any on you now, do you?"

Corinne laughed, and shoved him on the shoulder. "Wouldn't you like to know?" She finished her strawberry lemonade, scooted forward, and fell into the lake. She floated up, squealing. "What the hell is this? Glacial runoff?"

James sighed, finished his beer, left the bottle on the dock, and slid in after her. "No, but it is fed by mountain streams, and it's deep enough that only the top gets warm. The water stays nice and cold. Means we have quite a few species of fish, including trout, and fat and happy catfish running along the bottom. From what I've been told, we're having a catfish fry later on."

Corinne's face lit up. "With hush puppies?" she asked, referring to balls of fried cornmeal.

"And twisty fries. Gunny gave Rachael this curly fry cutter for Christmas, and she cuts some and he fries them up."

Corinne started circling James like a shark. "You getting along with Gunny now?"

James shrugged. "The man tried to apologize when I was thirteen, hurting and grief-stricken, unable to really hear a word that he said. Tried a couple of times to explain what the hell happened. When I was younger, I yelled at him or I shut down. When I got older, I took swings at him. I'm not terribly proud of my behavior, but there is a lot I couldn't hear then that I can hear now."

James walked into the lake and caught Corinne around the waist, but she wriggled out of his grasp and swam off. He followed her. They swam over to a canoe that had been upended. Gunny and Rachael lazily kissed in the water instead of climbing back in. James righted it and tried to give it back, but the happy couple completely ignored him. James put the paddles back in and towed it back to the dock. Corinne followed him. James tied it to the dock by throwing a loop around a docking cleat, and pulled himself out of the water. Corinne put her feet against the dock and held up her good hand, and James pulled her out. He carefully handed her into the boat, then ran to the end of the dock to the cooler, and put their empties in the recycling. He pulled out two cans of soda, and brought them back to the boat. "You know how to steer?" James asked Corinne. "You can be the rudder, and I'll paddle this like a kayak."

"I'll try anything once," said Corinne. His very strong arms pulled them forward, but she couldn't get the paddle back far enough to use her paddle like a true rudder, so she just paddled on one side or the other to steer. He got to the middle of the lake and just floated, and they both lay their paddles across the canoe in front of them.

James very slowly and carefully turned around in the canoe, and renewed their earlier conversation. "I spent a lot of time up on the mountain, thinking about things, but you're the one that got it through my skull that the situation was so horrible that no one could have done anything right, no matter what they did."

"It happened that way with one of my friends. Her dad..." James saw the flat look in her eyes, and his face twisted. She nodded, once. "She got away from him before...that happened. When her mother saw her dad in a state of half-undress chase her out of the house, things got even worse. Her dad went to jail, her mom committed suicide, and Tania went to live with her grandmother. All her mother's family was dead, and her grandmother was her father's mother. The grandma didn't believe that her little boy could've done such a terrible thing, and gaslighted my friend's brother into believing it too."

James quickly grasped the situation. "She couldn't throw a fit and end up in the foster system, get separated from her brother, whom I assume she was trying to protect. So she lost her father, her mother, her brother, and her grandmother all because of one man's horrible nature." He nodded his head once, hard. "So that's why you became the secret scholarship fund for your friends."

"They became my family, from the very first day. We were assigned the same dorm room, a triple, and after a fight over who got the top bunk, we were friends ever since." She grinned. "Kandace won the top bunk, until she got too drunk and fell out. Then I got it. Anyhow, Tania's father's lawyer couldn't get into the money set aside for her bachelor's degree, but he sure as hell tried to get the money for the graduate degree."

"Your friend's brother is still covered?" asked James. "We can set up another scholarship fund."

"No, I started a little fund, haven't touched it." She narrowed her eyes. "I sure wish Dana's brother was in treatment, like Tania's mother should have been. Dana says they've tried doing that with Rooney, but he won't take the medication for more than two or three days. That's not even time for him to actually have any side effects. He just doesn't think he's sick and needs any meds."

James nodded. "I can think of at least eight people who tried over the years to help Rooney. The man won't accept any. Some people you just can't help."

Corinne stared off to the other side of the lake, not really seeing the pine and oak trees, the crystal-blue sky, the rippling water, the fat fluffy clouds. "Tania is teaching in South Korea now. I get why she felt she had to leave the country. She has an apartment with all her health care paid for and she says she's paying off her loans really quickly. She says she could walk down the sidewalk at two in the morning and feel perfectly safe. I get the safe thing, I really do. But, it smashes my heart that we're in separate places. Looking at someone on a video screen is just not the same damn thing." She wiped tears from her eyes.

James reached over, took Corinne's good hand in his. "Let's follow her example, get you more clients, get everything paid off. Then, you can go visit her, wherever in the world she is. The same with your other friend, Kandace."

Corinne smiled a watery smile. "Don't even know where that girl is. She's keeping it on the down low." She wiped the tears from the corners of her eyes. "It's a gorgeous day, and we are supposed to be out here having fun. It's my first time swimming since that day on the mountain. I should be enjoying every minute of it. Instead, I got us all talking about serious things. I'm sorry, James. Apparently, I've forgotten how to have a good time."

James smiled at her, and carefully leaned forward to brush away her tears with the sides of his thumbs. "You never have to apologize for how you feel." He leaned back. "I have something I want to show you." He did a complicated turn without tipping the boat, then he paddled forward with quick strokes, and soon they were in a little cove.

There was a big, sturdy tree with a thick branch hanging over the water. So, of course there was a rope swing, one end tied to a thick tree branch, the other with a knot on the end hanging over the water. James hopped out and pulled the canoe onto the sand, slid both paddles into the canoe, and held out his hand to walk Corinne out of the boat. He pulled the canoe onto the bank. "This is a little dangerous for you. I can swing out with you and we can land on my back, or you can try it yourself and try to land on your good side, or point your toes and slide into the water." He held out a hand, and they walked up the small rise. "The water out here is really deep, but you're wearing a flotation device, so you won't drown unless some idiot lands on top of you."

Corinne laughed. "I'll watch for that. Let's jump together the first time. We can land on your ass instead of mine." James laughed, grabbed the rope, stood on it, brought her around in front of him, and stepped off the ledge. They both whooped as they flew out into the air, and they both let go at the same time. James held her tight around the waist, and fell backwards. They landed with a huge splash of water, and came up laughing and gasping. "Again!" screamed Corinne, and she started swimming to the shore. James laughed, and tried to keep up with her.

# CARE

unch involved a lot of grazing, with chips, veggies, dips, olives, crackers, several goat cheeses, and fruit salad. As people arrived, the snacks were replenished, and no one complained of hunger before dinner.

The sun was starting to go down when the fish fry started. The family fished from the family dock and from boats all along the lake and brought back both speckled and rainbow trout and catfish. As an expert, James was in charge of gutting and filleting the fish. Corinne gave him a wide berth during this process, choosing to hang out with Rachael and Stretcher, who were in charge of breading the fish and making hush puppies. The sunburned Mitch was in charge of cutting and breading the twisted fries. Corinne used tongs to get the egg-battered fish into Rachael's breading. Gunny stood ready in front of two vats of oil, tongs and fry baskets in hand, Rico there to assist.

Everyone stood back as the first plates went in, afraid of being splattered with hot oil. Then, it was a race to get the baskets out and dumped while everyone else readied the plates, tartar sauce, and sour cream dip, and Rachael sliced up some fruit for a salad. There were giant pitchers of sweet tea, strawberry lemonade, and iced coffee, along with cans of soda. They all stood and Rachael sang the thing about spirit. They sat at the giant picnic table, Gunny on one end, Rachael on the other, and passed the platters of food up and down. The dogs were under the table, ready to catch any fallen morsels.

Mitch was ready with tales of his prowess on the lake, including catching a string of catfish. Corinne had a cut lip from slipping and landing wrong at the rope swing, and everyone ribbed her about it. Jokes and risqué comments flew, and it was extremely common to see people doubled over with laughter.

Corinne was quick to note that the jokes were not aimed at Mitch, who sat beside her, or James, who sat across from her and to the left, about their living arrangements. No one seemed to care. Stretcher had already had her questions answered, and so didn't seem inclined to ask any more.

Corinne hadn't eaten food like that since Tania had taken her home to sample her grandmother's cooking several years before. Corinne ate as if no one was ever going to feed her again. She was startled to realize she cleaned her plate twice, and that plates with slivers of pecan, peach, apple, and plum pies, complete with a scoop of cinnamon ice cream, were being passed around the table. She had no idea how she did it, but Corinne inhaled all the pie slivers and ice cream. She lay back in her chair, disinclined to move. She groaned when she realized they were making the dish line again, and forced herself to stand next to Mitch and pass the plates on down. She used a wet wipe to clean her fingers when the last serving platters were passed down, stumbled toward the porch, found an Andirondack chair, and fell into it.

Mitch sat down next to her, smiling. "Helluva day, isn't it?"

James came over with two cans of soda. He pushed one can into the top of her flotation vest, which she still wore to hold her arm still. He popped the top on the other can and put it in her hand. She groaned with pleasure at the cold hitting her abused shoulder. "Hey! Don't I get one?" Mitch asked his brother.

James narrowed his eyes at Mitch. "If you have been thinking about something other than yourself, you may have realized that

Corinne here swam for the first time since she was assaulted today, and her shoulder probably hurts like hell."

Mitch grinned at his brother insouciantly. "Well, we have you to think of things like that."

James knelt, and looked his brother in the eye. "I just spent four days out of the house. Did you think of any of that at all while I was gone?"

Mitch scowled, then realized what he was doing. He stilled his face.

Corinne looked over at him. "I can see the wheels turning in your head. You know damn well you didn't do more than check on me once or twice a day over the entire four days." She smiled gently at James. "Why not get a soda for yourself and your brother, and pull up another chair?" Corinne pointed to an empty chair. "You better snag it before it gets gone."

"Good idea," said James. He stood, moved the chair over, and went to go get the sodas.

"I know what you're going to say," said Mitch. "Twelve-year-olds think only of themselves, and not about anyone else." He stole a sip of her cola, and swallowed hard. "And, you're absolutely right. I was a jackass. I asked you to come upstairs with me more than once, not thinking about the fact that we needed to get a new damn railing."

"Already ordered it," said James, who had come back from snagging the drinks. He handed Mitch his own can, and popped the top of his soda. "Measured everything twice. And, I apologize, because it hasn't come in yet. Would have installed it two weeks ago if it had."

"I have to start thinking of things like that." Mitch grimaced. "And, I did exactly what I wanted to today, and never checked in with either one of you."

James grinned, then got a serious look on his face. "We had lots of fun, but I overtired and injured Corinne here. I was kind of an ass. I thought about short term fun and not about long-term recovery."

Corinne groaned. "Please don't remind me, because I was just as much of an ass, but toward myself. I'm sore as hell. And, I'm sorry to say, I'm probably only going to make it as far as the bathroom, possibly my desk, but more likely I'm going to move everything back to the recliner to work. If one of you could move my laptop, I'd greatly appreciate it."

"I'll do it. Thank goodness for the dictation software." James made a note on his phone.

"Truth," said Corinne. "So, what happens next at these shindigs? Do Gunny and Rachael pull out baby pictures? Show slides of all of your vacations?"

Both Mitch and James doubled over laughing. "What do you think, we live in the seventies?" asked James.

Mitch snorted. "No, no. Something much cooler. I don't know if it's *Battlestar Galactica, Firefly,* or *Killjoys.* Sometimes it's *Alien* and *Aliens.* Or a selection of superhero movies."

"We are going to have to wait on the popcorn because we don't actually want to make it ourselves," said James.

"I'm ready to pop now," said Corinne, cradling her stomach.

"We will wait until after the first movie. Butter, cheddar cheese, caramel, and jalapeno popcorn, and the regular kind with mini M&Ms in it. And all the sugary sodas we can drink," James said, holding up his can of cola.

"We sleep in sleeping bags on the floor, if the sugar high wears off," said Mitch.

"But you're special, and will get one of the recliners." James pointed at Corinne's sore arm with his can.

"Unless you want to go home," said Mitch. "Then we'll get on the road right away."

James made a popping noise by putting his finger in his mouth and pulling on his cheek. "You know what that sound was?" James asked Mitch.

Mitch sighed. "The sound of my head popping out of my ass. I know."

Corinne laughed, and then groaned as she accidentally moved her shoulder, and felt her split lip threaten to split again. "Quit making me laugh. Hurts."

Stretcher stuck her head out the door. "Check your texts. Vote, and we'll get started. Dishes are almost done. I already staked out the recliner on the left for Corinne. Anyone sits in it, they die." She popped her head back and closed the door.

They split their vote; Mitch voted for *Firefly* and James and Corinne for *Battlestar Galactica*. They all lost, and came in to find *Iron Man's* opening credits playing. Mitch made sure Corinne was settled in on the recliner, James went for more drinks, and they all settled in to watch the movies. The family's running commentary made Corinne gasp in pain from laughing so hard, and Mitch went out to the truck to get her pills for her. She dozed a bit during the third movie, her pills making her sleepy. But, she woke up for the popcorn tasting contest, and found that she liked the caramel kind and the kind with the tiny M&Ms in it the best. She fell asleep near the end of the fourth movie, and everybody went to sleep themselves after the fifth one.

In the morning, they had crispy bacon, fat sage-infused sausages, cheese grits with butter, and peach juice. Rachael said, "Let's get you some pills. I'll put a movie on, or you can read a book."

"Shifter conference," James explained. "We are going to change and do a run, and be back in a few hours. Will that be okay with you? I can sit this one out if you..."

Corinne held up a hand. "I'll probably snooze again, to be honest. The idea of getting in the truck and bouncing around on the back roads horrifies me."

"We brought your toiletries kit." Mitch put the case down on the little table next to the recliner. He hung a small black backpack on the hook under the edge of the table. "You've got shorts, underwear, and an XL shirt in there. There is a full bath off to the right. You want one of us to stay while you take a shower?"

Corinne laughed. "I was an ice-cold, freshwater lake for half the day yesterday. I think I'm clean enough." She waved at both of them. "Go. Be free. If you love me, you'll come back to me. If not, it just wasn't meant to be," she said in an incredibly dramatic voice.

Mitch, James, and Rachael all burst out in surprised laughter, and

Stretcher coughed. "I like this one," said Rachael. "If either one of you screws this up, no more fish frys for you."

Both Mitch and James looked at her in horror. "You wouldn't," said James.

"Try me." Rachael narrowed her eyes.

"Stop making me laugh," said Corinne, clutching her injured shoulder. They had managed to get the stretchy band contraption off of her, and she was wearing her regular sling.

"Ice pack," said James.

"Cold soda," said Mitch. They both turned to get the items she needed.

Stretcher raised her eyebrows. "Wow. I can see the benefits."

Corinne grinned at her. "I've never had people rushing to please me before. I could get used to this."

Mitch came back with a small cooler, loaded with both ice packs and several drinks. James came back with a small sandwich, which he slid into the top of the cooler. "If we're not back in time, eat up. But keep it light, because we're going to have one hell of a lunch."

"Make your own mini pizzas. Cheddar, beef, and red onion." Mitch patted his belly.

"Bacon, mushroom, black olive, and Italian sausage," said James.

"Make me one of those when you get back. James' kind. Now, shoo. I want to go back to sleep." Corinne waved the back of her hand at them.

"Demanding, isn't she?" said Mitch, making her laugh, then groan again. And then, they were gone.

# STORM

The storm crashed down from everywhere. Lightning leapt from cloud to cloud, and from the sky to the ground. The sky was gunmetal-gray mixed with inky black, the rain coming down in sheets.

Corinne has suggested that they install a dog door large enough for a wolf. Mitch had scoffed, which was strange because he was the one that liked to turn himself into a wolf-dog and roam the property and the mountain. James actually built the thing. It wasn't as hard as it would seem because the door was already in panels. He just cut two panels out and installed heavy rubber sheeting with a magnet on the end, and installed a strip of metal under the door. Mitch whined, both as a human and a dog, about using a damn dog door, but he soon changed whenever he wanted, then went in and out whenever he pleased. No water seemed to be coming in from the dog door; Corinne was relieved.

Corinne worked madly, because she knew damn well the power was going to go out. They had solar power and quite a few sunny days, so there was quite a bit stored, and a backup generator. But, it was those critical moments of transition that could cause her to lose some of her work. She had just created a total of eleven ads for a new client, inserted the pictures, copied and corrected URLs, and set the times and places to get them all up and running when there was a huge burst of thunder that made her jump. She made sure everything she had done was backed up to the computer's battery backup system as the lightning flashed so brightly that she had to cover her eyes.

She opened them wide as Blackie/Mitch entered through the dog door, something in his mouth. He lay a bedraggled puppy on her foot. "Oh, baby!" she said, and immediately picked up the puppy. Corinne rushed to the laundry room, pulled out a small towel, still warm from the dryer, and wiped down the puppy. It seemed to be a corgi. She looked at the muddy paws and was about to head to the bathroom when Blackie came in again with another puppy in his mouth. She wrapped up the first one in the towel and put it down, and then picked up the second one. The first one was dead silent and breathing raggedly, but the second one was crying. "It's okay, baby," she said, getting the water out of its eyes and holding it close. The puppy licked her hand, and she melted.

Corinne decided to stay put long enough to see if there were more puppies. She pulled down a laundry basket, grabbed another towel and put the wrapped puppies in it. Blackie came in with two more, and Corinne was running out of towels. "Any more?" she asked, and Blackie went back out into the storm, came back in, and dropped the fifth one at her feet. Blackie sat, and she said, "Turn yourself into a human and get in the shower with these puppies. They need to be cleaned and to get warm."

The transformation only took a few seconds of blurred brightness. Mitch slowly stood as a man from his position on the floor. "Follow me." Corinne put the fifth dog in the basket, put large clean towels over her shoulder, picked up the laundry basket, and went to the downstairs shower. Mitch didn't say a word as he turned on the shower to lukewarm. Mitch stepped in, Corinne passed in puppy after puppy, and Mitch washed each one with the hypoallergenic shampoo she used to clean her hair buildup. Corinne dried them all, lined the laundry basket with an old blanket from the hall closet, and checked the puppies over for injuries. There didn't seem to be any outward damage. There were two girls and three boys, and their eyes were open. "Thank Spirit. I really didn't feel like waking up every two hours to feed them."

Corinne left a still-silent Mitch in the shower, and brought the puppies into the kitchen by balancing the laundry basket on her hip. She took some baked chicken and some plain white rice out of the refrigerator, cut up the chicken, and mixed in the rice. She grabbed a handful of cut-up carrots, put them in the microwave, and zapped them until they were soft. She put the chicken, rice, and carrots into the blender, and mixed it all up. She then divided the food into five small plastic bowls, put them on the floor, sat on the floor, and took each dog out and put the puppy in front of a bowl. She filled up two larger plastic bowls full of water, and put a plastic liner under some paper she found in the recycling bin. The runt was a little girl, and Corinne fed that puppy by hand.

Corinne got them fed and watered, and put them on the piddle paper. Some of them piddled, some didn't. She put them back in their laundry basket, and held them close, one by one. They licked her fingers and her face, and made little squeaking noises as they wandered about their new environment. She changed the newspaper she was using for a piddle pad, washed up, and came back to sit with the puppies.

Mitch sat on the floor and took a dog with one hand, and showed her his mobile phone with the other. "I ordered puppy chow, toys, blankets, a baby gate, pet cleaning spray, and bowls for all of them. Finding homes for them actually won't be a problem because corgis are excellent herding dogs."

Corinne looked shocked. Mitch looked into Corinne's eyes. "You can have the runt and maybe one other, but we can't have five dogs here. They are not large dogs like labs or goldens that James can take with them on his hikes. They're working dogs, and need jobs to feel safe, secure, and happy." He took back the phone, sent another text, and put the phone into the shorts he now wore, post-shower. His hair curled around his shoulders, still wet. He looked down at the bowls. "You were smart about the chicken, rice, and carrots. That'll be fine until the order shows up tomorrow. Doc Anderson will take such good care of them. She's the best vet in three counties, and will get their dog books and immunization schedule straightened out tomorrow."

Corinne looked over at Mitch, put the runt down, stroked his arm, then picked up another dog. "You saw something horrible, didn't you? Your eyes look... haunted."

"Some idiot abandoned them in a holler. The mom drowned trying to get them to safety. I couldn't get to her in time. I heard the puppies crying, and had a hell of a time bringing them over one by one. That's why they're so damn bedraggled. I wish I could have done it faster, but I can't call anyone on a cell phone as a dog, so my cell phone is upstairs. The change takes time, and I didn't have time to waste. Besides, as a human I would have smelled strange to them, and I would've been naked besides. This way, they simply perceived me as another dog and didn't fight me."

He changed dogs, snuggling with one of the girls this time. "She slipped away so fast. I thought I had her, but she went under. I went in after her, but by the time I dragged her out she was gone." Tears streamed down his face, and Corinne held him close. He cried a little, and they kept up their holding-dogs vigil. Corinne got peed on, but her shirt was so wet and muddy by that point it didn't faze her a bit.

Mitch brought Corinne a new shirt and shorts. Corinne changed clothes. They made it over to the couch, put the basket between them, and ended up cuddling the dogs. Two ended up on Mitch's lap, one in between them, and both the girls ended up with Corinne. Corinne completely forgot about doing anything related to work. She kept stroking the dogs and sending them into little doggy raptures. They watched a ridiculous comedy neither one of them remembered when it was over, and they both fell asleep on the couch.

They fell into a routine. They slept either on the couch or in Mitch's bed, the puppies all around, in their hair, on their necks, cuddled in their arms. Mitch began working when the sun cracked the horizon, trying to get all of his work out so that Corinne could do hers. Corinne did her work with the puppy box at her feet, at least one puppy on her lap. She ordered an infant carrier, and had at least one puppy in it at all times when she was working. Mitch quit his rambling as a dog, content to stay home and make sure the puppies were all right.

~

*R*achael came down with the vegetables on her usual day, entered the back door after a knock, hurriedly put her basket down, and rushed over to see the puppies. "Oh, my stars! What happened to the mother?"

Corinne tried not to cry when telling her the news. "Mitch was outside as Blackie, and couldn't save the abandoned mother from drowning."

"That's horrible. My poor Mitch!"

"He cried in my hair. The puppies did, too."

"I take it this was the night of the storm?"

"The very same. I'm holding the runt, Sheila, and we have Shawn, Wayne, Rascal, and Lucy." Corinne grinned. "The girls sleep in my hair at night, and on my lap when we're in front of the TV on the couch. The vet said the puppies are damn lucky to have been found during the storm, and ranted against whoever would abandon the corgi and her puppies during a rainstorm."

Rachael got a flat look in her eyes. "I won't go into my own rant, but you can guess what I would say. And most of it in very bad language, which I can't repeat in front of the children." Rachael picked up Wayne in one hand and Shawn and the other, and laughed when she was smothered with puppy kisses. "Oh, my stars. We'll adopt all three boys. Corgis are very special. They just need to learn some whistles, and they'll help us around the farm." She looked up at Corinne. "We are now responsible for those three, with their medical care and all. How old did the vet say that they are?"

"They open their eyes in ten days, but they didn't cry and root around for food. I am damn lucky that I guessed right on their age, that they could have regular food. I could've killed these puppies by thinking they were weaned when they weren't." Rachael and Corinne both cringed at the thought. "They are three, nearly four weeks old. The vet suggested keeping them together until they are six weeks old. The problem is that I'm super-attached to them all. Sean gets into everything, Wayne and Rascal fight with each other all the time, Sheila is a sweetie, and Lucy plays the so-sad card to try to get more food or petting."

Rachael laughed. "You're an excellent dog mom." She traded Wayne for Rascal. "So, I'm super-excited. We'll get dogs in two weeks!"

Corinne said, "I don't quite know how to talk about this, but I have some questions. Will the dogs get nervous about predators in the house?"

Rachael shook her head. "Unlike Mitch, we generally go quite far away from the house before we change. And, if you're worried about Stretcher, she generally waits until she's high up on the mountain to change. And, she gets along with Mitch in both forms, so I don't think she'll have a problem with the pups. If she does, she can always move out to one of the outbuildings. We actually have rooms over the barn. We're thinking of putting apartments or possibly even tiny houses farther out." She smiled a little sadly, as she switched out Wayne for Shawn. "Not to buy into a stereotype, but shifters are often loners. If they get around too many people they freak out. They do like the occasional get-together. I hold them as often as they can stand, call them in for cookouts followed by meetings. We give people time to run free together. Or feathered, if they're that type. I know of some scaled ones, too."

Corinne's eyes got huge. "Any alligators?"

"I really hope not." Rachael winced. "Alligators and dogs don't get along so well."

Corinne traded Sheila for Lucy, and installed the dog in the carrier. Sheila cried piteously, and Rachael laughed and picked her up. "This one is getting spoiled. And bigger. I can tell she's the runt, but she's catching up with her siblings." Rachael looked around. "Where is James? I haven't seen him since last week."

"Neither have we. He put in nearly a week straight. We hope to see him later on today." The dogs started barking and Lucy gave a little howl because they heard the vehicle drive up. "He's early."

James came in the back door, talking. "Mitch won't even say hi to me. What's up with..." He looked at Rachael and Corinne sitting on the floor, and he dropped his backpack on the ground. "Puppies!" he said, and his whole face lit up. He came over, set cross-legged on the floor, and Corinne introduced him to all the puppies.

Corinne kissed James' cheek. "Your brother had a tough time, losing the mother in the storm," she said quietly against his ear.

Rachael stood, retrieved the produce basket and hauled it to the sink, and grabbed a handful of purple carrots. "I'll get the veggies washed and sorted. You meet your new family, James. We've got dibs on the boys, but you get the girls."

"Wait a minute! I want a boy, too!" James picked them up, one by one, petted and exclaimed over them, and debated keeping a boy as well as Sheila or Lucy with Corinne. Rachael smiled to herself, and texted Gunny that she needed to stop by the pet store on the way home.

~

*M*itch went on a ride the same day Rachael came to pick up the puppies—the males, because Lucy and Sheila were so firmly imprinted on Corinne. Despite bonding over having to take Corinne to physical therapy, Mitch had been nearly silent for weeks. James had four lieu days, so they sent Mitch off on a camping trip with Stretcher and Jared with hugs and kisses from Corinne and a hug and shoulder slap from James. They watched him ride away. "If keeping all five puppies would help Mitch talk, I'd do that." James' voice was heavy with worry. "But, that doesn't seem to be it, or directly it, anyway."

"Do you think he's worried that he won't see them often? He and Gunny at least seem to be able to enter the same backyard together."

"Yeah, if each are on diagonal corners."

"So, not it."

"No. I think the corgi he couldn't save reminded him of Mom. And Dad."

Corinne reached out, touched James' hand. "Issues."

"Grab a tissue, and cry it out." James finished the joke. "He's always kept it inside."

"And became a porcupine." They went back into the house. Lucy and Sheila valiantly tried to hop over the sill of their play box.

James barked a laugh. "Yeah, with flying quills." He pretended to duck a quill.

Corinne laughed, and shut the door behind them. "I'll make the sandwiches. You get their dog bowls, food, and bottled water."

"On it." James moved to get the dog things into the smaller backpack Corinne could sling over her good shoulder James carried the heavier backpack with the human food, water, snacks, drinks, and blanket.

They got it all packed, and James made sure Corinne had everything she needed—hiking boots, sling so she didn't move her arm the wrong way, sunblock, and mosquito repellent. She was nearly healed, but it seemed prudent to put on a sling for a hike. He put sunblock and repellent on them both, made sure the dogs had eaten and gotten enough water, and double-checked all the packing. He put the lighter backpack on Corinne, shouldered the heavier one, and readied the dog slings. They would be carried probably twice to three times as much as they would walk. Corinne got Lucy because she cried for her mommy, and James got Sheila. They got their walking sticks, and he walked them to the trailhead.

The hike was flat, with only a few small rises. They went through the forest, light filtering through the trees along the way. The puppies attacked errant leaves and spots of sunlight. They found the meadow, bright with sunlight, butterflies in blue, white, and orange, a carpet of little white and blue flowers on the ground. James found a flat place with close-cropped grass, checked for anthills, then shook out the blanket. The dogs explored while they laid out the dog bowls with their drinking water. The dogs chased butterflies, which made Corinne laugh.

"It is so awesome to see you laugh. And to see you move the arm."

Corinne cradled her left arm in her right, then slowly extended her arm. She hissed. "Pisses me off. The pain is the muscles, ligaments, all that not wanting to move after being locked in one place for so long. 'I don't want to mooove!' " whined Corinne, pretending her arm could talk.

James laughed. "Let me help you." He helped her stretch out her arm in a small range of motion. He stopped when sweat broke out on her forehead. He put the sling back on her. "Woman, you would work yourself until you're screaming because you're tough as nails."

Corinne said, "I don't have squat to prove. I thought I did, 'cause Tania and Kandace are ten times stronger than me in vastly different ways. But, not so much now." She stood, hissing, and went to stand in front of a fallen log she saw in between the trees. The dogs gamely followed her. Corinne stood back, called the puppies to her, and got a knife out of a hidden pocket in her shorts. She let the small, flat knife fly, and it stuck hard in the wood.

"Damn, girl." James retrieved the knife, cleaned it, and gave it back. "You rock."

"I can only hit the bulls-eye five out of ten. Got to six out of ten last week, then the physical therapy set me back." She slid the knife back in its sheath, and they walked back to the picnic blanket.

"Pain takes some active physical memory. Kind of like having too many windows open on a computer. The rest of your physicality gets kind of slower while processing it. The body is also trying to keep you from hurting yourself further. That's what pain is."

Corinne got her pills out, popped two, and swallowed them down with water. She put the box away. "I am so sick of needing pills to get through the day. But, the doctor says I'm doing really well, a week or two early. Feel good about that, but I can't lift weights. Can't even put a weight on my stomach during sit-ups in case it falls the wrong way. I love high-intensity interval training, but even low-impact where I have one foot on the ground..."

"I know what low-impact means."

Corinne pretended to take a swing at James, thwarted by puppy bodies getting in between them. "The point is, jiggling the shoulder around at all makes me scream and sweat much more than usual."

"We can do flat hikes like this. Get you and the little ones out of the house. Just have to be careful not to fall into any gopher holes."

Corinne grimaced. "That would really suck. I miss the boys, but having five dogs underfoot was tricky. You both caught me several times. With them growing up, I admit keeping all five would have been an accident waiting to happen."

They petted the dogs, and watched them run around. James told Corinne about his most recent hike, with six bickering college friends who slipped in and out of each other's tents. "They did not."

James held up two fingers. "Scout's honor," he said, making her laugh. "There was a gay couple, a lesbian couple, and two who were oblivious to the whole thing. It seems old memories overcame them."

"Did anyone stay together after the hike?"

"There was a clear announcement that the gay couple was together. Everyone cheered. The lesbians talked about moving closer to each other, so maybe on that one."

"Yay!" said Corinne, and clapped her hands. The puppies thought she was calling them and came running. James and Corinne took turns throwing a rag with a knot tied in the middle for the girls so they could chase and tug at it, and tumble over each other to get to it.

"I need sustenance." Corinne pointed to the picnic basket.

"What did you pack?" James reached for the basket.

"Chicken salad with grapes and almonds, olive bread, strawberries, and sparkling cherry water."

"Yum." James spread out a blanket, and took out the goodies. They ate, drank, and fed tiny bits of the chicken to the dogs. James cleaned up, then he lay back on his pack. Corinne lay her head on his stomach, Sheila climbed up James like he was a mountain, and Corinne scooped up Lucy. James stroked Corinne's hair with one hand, and Sheila's head and soft ears with the other. "Corinne?"

"Hmm?"

"Are you okay, really? With the whole shapeshifter thing. The whole being a family thing."

"The sleeping with two brothers thing. Splitting my love." She opened one eye.

He tilted his head down. "Really? Do you hear any objections?"

She closed her eye again. "I get two men who love me, who want me to be happy. You both are so...self-sufficient, I guess. A few sandwiches and sodas and you're good. You both pick up after yourselves, and I can use the fuzzy duster thingy and the vacuum now, so I can do my chores. Switch the laundry over. Folding things and hanging things up, not so much, but it's very late summer and we don't hang much up. Cleaning up after five dogs was annoying, but you both stepped up like you always do."

"Back atcha with the self-sufficient. Every day you try to do a little bit more. It's maddening, actually. I love you, and want to do stuff for you, like folding the laundry and putting it away. I can do some of it on my lieu days. But, you guys get stuff delivered."

"Jack. He's the delivery guy. There's an app. He says he gets his car and insurance payment the first two weeks, and spends the rest of the month paying his rent, bills, and two online college classes. Kid wants to be an X-ray tech. Says he's getting rid of what he calls his baby classes like math and English composition so he can start full-time next year."

"Tall kid, glasses, dark hair?" Corinne grunted in affirmation. "He's a smart kid. Rachael uses him to send produce all over the county if Gunny is using the delivery truck for something else."

"What the hell does Gunny do?"

James laughed. "Other than farming and raising goats?" He laughed again. "He teaches heirloom farming classes online. People from as far away as Cameroon and Bosnia have taken his course. He and Rachael are all for the preservation of seeds and bioagricultural diversity. Gunny has two degrees himself."

Corinne nodded. "Can he turn into a... what? Giant dog? Wolf?"

"Both, and, like me, finds shifting into a coyote impossible."

"Can I see your wolf?"

James stilled his hands, then resumed stroking both woman and puppy. "I find it to be really private, you know that. It's great in an emergency. I can find missing hikers using my nose. Saves us time for having to call for trained dogs and get them out to a remote site." He laughed. "You were Mitch's first rescue. He was so proud of that." His hands stilled again. "Until the night of the rainstorm."

"He's torn up inside. I've tried to reach him, but..."

"He's gone all brick-wall on me too. He's always been moody, and very angry, but this is....sad."

"Good. Maybe he's gotten past his anger to the point where he can be sad."

"I never thought of it that way. He was holding onto his anger, but now he sees how juvenile that is. He's letting the anger go, and all the shit he held back with the anger is flooding in." James thought a minute. "I would go after him, have a talk, but being away is what he needs right now, I think. Away from you and the puppies. He needs to clear his head."

"You're a good brother." Corinne held James' hand.

James snorted. "Not hardly. We were so young when our parents died, and the whole thing happened in such a horrible way. We both went nuts, I think, and your arrival seems to have unknotted a twisted rope, one knot at a time. I want mine gone, because I can see that it stands in my way. Mitch holds onto his, thinking he'll disappear without being all twisted." He bent over, and kissed Corinne. "You, love, have unknotted me." He lay back, and stroked her hair.

"I was so determined to do this alone." Corinne stroked James' hand while Lucy fell asleep in the crook of her arm. "Pay everybody off. Work sixteen hours a day, I guess. But things are getting paid off much faster, even with me paying a third of everything, paying off the Harley. I was gonna do some work with Mitch, learn his business too, but then this happened." She moved her arm a tad, and hissed. "So, that got sidetracked. But, I took that Internet marketing course for specialized industries, and now I've got niches. Bookstores, coffee shops, authors. I even have an employee to do the stuff that can be nearly automated, but needs a human to set up, keep running. I can concentrate on big honking websites, and the smaller specialized ones. And Dana does the photos, lovely work. A little PhotoShop, and they're good to go. And so, I pay big honking payments, get things gone," she said smugly.

"You built a company, all by yourself. Hardly a group effort. You picked and trained Dana, too. Impressive."

"I did. But, it's the other stuff. Not just the laundry, or taking care of me 'cause I'm winged. No, it's another Coke when I'm bashing out a website. A back rub when I hunch over too much. A foot rub while watching some silly movie to reset my brain so I can think again. It's...laughter. I've never laughed so much in my life, even with Tania and Kandace."

"We're a family." James kissed her hair. "I have chicken salad and crackers, and taking the dogs for walks and playing with them. And movies to reset my brain, too. Sex. Joyful sex. Fun sex. We don't have to think about it, we just do it, and it's..."

"Amazing."

"Amazing." James kissed her.

"Not in front of the children," said Corinne. James lay back and groaned. Corinne laughed.

# REUNION

*C*orinne and James spent two days in bed, the dogs asleep on the bathroom rug, back in bed with them when the clothes went back on. He sucked, kissed, and licked her. He tasted her, her tongue, skin, lips, thighs, and the part of her that made her want to buck and scream. She wanted him even more than he wanted her. James had to threaten to stop all sexual activity if she didn't leave her sling on. She wanted to touch and taste him, too.

After puppy baths, James gave Corinne baths. Long ones, where he washed and conditioned her hair, washed her all over, and let her soak. He'd wash himself, sweaty after doing all the house chores he could find, including fixing faucet leaks and installing the exceptionally late-delivery banister. The hanging-in-midair stairs had looked exceptionally cool when they'd installed them several years ago after tearing out the rotted ones from the old two-story house. But now they were just unsafe, and much too high for corgi legs. The corgis would cry if left alone downstairs all night, so they had to be carried up and down stairs. James increased the number of stairs, made them shallower, and installed the new railing.

After his shower after another long day of house chores, James sat in the tub with Corinne. "Camping is the weirdest, in some ways." He held Corinne close as the puppies slept on the fuzzy bathroom rug.

"How? Tent, fire, songs and stories. Cooking hot dogs on sticks. Easy."

"Well, I can't tell you how many people hike and are shocked when it's muddy, or rocky." Corinne laughed. "A lot of people come up to have sex, and the tent falls on them." Corinne guffawed, then groaned as she laughed too hard. "We do have bears, real ones, not shapeshifters. People leave their food out, and are surprised when bears show up to eat it. They can't fathom why I hang the food in a tree. Then, there's the kids. Scared of every noise, and a lot of them have never even been without a night light before, and the dark of the woods is nearly absolute."

"What do you do?"

"Well, I don't tell them ghost stories like their idiot parents. I always carry the fixing for s'mores. A little chocolate, graham crackers, and melted marshmallows, and everyone is happy." He grinned. "I've also got a program on my phone, shows the constellations. I get them looking at the stars, and they're fine." He kissed Corinne's ear. "Lots of people canoe the rivers and lakes. There are white waters in some of 'em. Some like the rush. Me, I'm getting too old for that."

"I'd like to go canoeing when I'm better."

"Maybe we can get kayaks for Rachael and Gunny's lake." James made a satisfied sound deep in his throat. "Looks like I know what I'm getting the family for Christmas. Hell, I can start on it now. Gunny and Rachael would get a kick out of a little boathouse."

James was silent for a while, then he talked about his first love, Jeannie King, and her ability to climb like a goat. "Killed in a rockfall about two years ago. She was one of the best free climbers in the country. She left me at a trailhead when we broke up and said we weren't on the same trail." Corinne brushed his tears away.

Corinne told him about Tania, her courage, her refusal to let her early life destroy her, her attempts to remain in touch with her brother. "My heart just bleeds for her, but she just says, 'If life were fair, it would be called something else, like Heaven or The Wicked Get Punished Land." Corinne laughed. "She just uses that bright brain to solve some other obstacle in her way. Now Kandace...we really thought we were going to lose her. She was always wild. Like that perfect girl you see out of the corner of your eye on campus, and poof, she's gone. She could drink anyone in any fraternity or sorority under the table. But, even when she was a hellion, she would listen to Tania if Tania told her to behave or apologize. Says Tania eliminated half of what would have been her amends list when she sobered up."

Corinne grinned. "She says she's still sober. I hope this find-herself thing works out for her. She was a little lost when it was time to graduate. I know she saw college as her cocoon. But we all have to fly away." She barked out a laugh. "Except me. I got winged. Didn't fly so far."

James kissed each knuckle, starting with the one attached to her bad arm, making sure the arm was carefully supported in the water. "Really? Seems to me that you started your own business, with no one else's help. You have one employee already. Two, if you count Jack the delivery guy." Corinne laughed. "Also, you are funny, sweet, smart, and you refuse to take guff from anyone, including my prickly brother. You fought off a senseless attack, you escaped and made it down a mountain severely injured, you worked through the pain, you developed new skills, you..."

"Got seduced by silver-talking mountain men."

James barked out a laugh. "Most of the time, I'm talking to myself. Even if someone's with me, I'm just a guide, or someone who answers their questions. The one who builds rock walls and bushwhacks trails."

"You find lost little boys."

"That was an aberration. Kid slid down into a ravine and couldn't get back up, and no one could hear him yelling for help except me."

"You. In wolf form."

"I got large-dog for him. Crawled up on my belly. He actually got on my back. Do you believe that?"

"And walked him back up a switchback to his parents, with him saying 'Giddyup, doggie!' all the way."

James kissed the knuckles of her other hand. "Sorry, apparently I'm repeating my stories."

Corinne laughed. "I like them. Very soothing." She kissed him. "Now, have sex with me before this water turns cold."

"Yes, ma'am," said James. He then did exactly as he was told.

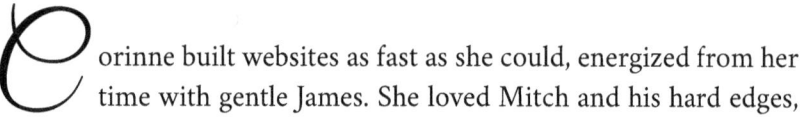

*M*itch came back from his long Harley ride, and instead of the happy, laid-back guy they had hoped for, he came back even more tight-lipped and sullen. Even Lucy and Sheila failed to move him. He threw himself into an extremely difficult custom build, one that would net him, supposedly, enough money for the entire year. He got up at dawn and came in at midnight, and took long, rambling walks when he needed a break. There was more than one thrown wrench, and he let go with streams of curse words Corinne hadn't heard strung together in that order. James had to go on two back-to-back hikes, so he called Jack and told him to call Corinne once a day to see if she needed anything, and told him to ask her to charge everything through the app. "Sure, man," said Jack. "I'm happy to do it. Earn me some green to pay for fall classes. Got me the two for summer all sewn up."

"You take care of her real good, and I'll tip you myself. You call Rachael down at the farm if you can't get to her, or she needs more stuff. Rachael will take care of it."

"On it, guide dude. You have a really good day now." James signed off, grinned, and headed off to be a "guide dude."

*C*orinne built websites as fast as she could, energized from her time with gentle James. She loved Mitch and his hard edges, but he was in full razor-wire porcupine mode. He wouldn't eat anything Corinne or Rachael made for him, he spoke in grunts as if he'd lost the power of speech, and he didn't kiss, hug, or touch Corinne at all.

Corinne didn't much like being ignored. It was hard to keep the house clean with two puppies, and Mitch had even given up folding the laundry. Corinne called Stretcher to take her to her physical therapy appointments, with knife-throwing before the physical therapy because Corinne was wiped out and in huge amounts of pain afterward.

Stretcher found out that Mitch hadn't given Corinne a hot bath after her physical therapy appointments both times that week. Corinne followed Stretcher into Mitch's workshop and watched, leaned her good arm against a wall. "What the hell crawled up your ass and died?" Stretcher asked Mitch.

Mitch finished tightening the nut on the bike he was working on, a job with a lot of chrome. He stood, and turned. "What the fuck, cat?"

Stretcher walked up to him, got in his face. "Your woman went to physical therapy on Monday and Thursday. It's Monday again. You haven't drawn her a hot bath, cleaned up the damn floor, or folded the laundry. Or fed or watered the puppies, or changed their piddle pads. Corinne has tried feeding you, and you won't eat. She's worried and in a lot of pain, and you haven't bothered to pop your head out of your ass long enough to help her. Your brother can't do it all. In case you haven't figured it out, he's got his own shit to do. Now, are you going to help out your woman, or not?"

In a non-response, Mitch walked around Stretcher and got on his bike. "Don't go," said Corinne, coming up behind Stretcher, in a voice that carried in the still, hot air. "If you go, you damage us." Mitch gave her a flat stare, and rode off.

Stretcher threw up her hands. "Come on. I can't carry you and your stuff, and the dogs and their stuff, so I'll have to call Rachael. She's going to be so pissed."

"Call...for what? And where am I going?"

"The farm. You don't need much help, but you can't go without it at all. If you slipped on dog pee and fell, James would kill Mitch. Then he would go all homicidal on me for not noticing there was a problem." Stretcher walked in the back door, and stepped over first one puppy, then the other one. "Let's get this place packed up."

Corinne walked to her laptop and started the unplugging process. "Good. Works for me."

~

*J*ames came home five days later, exhausted, with a huge scratch down one arm and a puncture wound in his thigh. A hiker had decided to have a screaming argument with his wife where the trail met the sky on the right side. Distracted, the man went over the edge, and the wife had, intelligently, grabbed him while simultaneously throwing herself down on the ground. James had caught her feet, crawled over her body, and grabbed the fallen hiker's other hand. They got him back up, but they had all been scratched by brush and twigs clinging to the hillside. James had given all three of them first aid, and everyone wanted the hike to continue.

It was the silent female in back, the friend and ex-lover of the other two, who had taken a sharpened stick and attacked the man around the campfire. James had been stabbed in the leg, but had gotten the stick out of her hand and wrestled the screaming woman to the ground. James tied her up with twine, the kind used to attach tent stakes. James let her go when the other two said they wouldn't be pressing charges.

The crazy woman took a flashlight, made it down to the trailhead, and stole the couple's car, leaving her own. James had to drive the couple to the police station to press charges, give his own statement, then drive the couple to the bus station to get home. He got four stitches in his thigh at the urgent care, and was pissed, sore, exhausted, and filthy. He didn't see Mitch or his bike, which was disturbing, because Mitch should have been in charge of watching over Corinne.

He was even more disturbed to find no trace of the dogs or Corinne, except for a faint scent of dog pee. Her laptop was gone, a duffel and her favorite shorts and tops were also missing. Mitch was not working on his Harley, either. There were no cut-up vegetables in the fridge, and all the dog food and pee pads were gone, too. James wrapped plastic wrap around his leg, took a shower, and scrubbed every inch of himself except the puncture wound, which the doctor at the urgent care center had cleaned and dressed. He checked his phone, and there was—finally!—a message. *Rachael put me in the new outbuilding. Puppies on my feet. We miss you. Come and get us. Bring us home.*

James sagged with relief. He'd doubted Corinne would run off. Mitch was squirrelly as hell, but Corinne? She was steady, reliable. He cleaned out the smelly, muddy SUV, put a load of laundry in the washer and turned it on. Then he got in the SUV and drove it the opposite direction from Rachael and Gunny's farm to the car wash he'd seen flyers for on the way in, for a school trip to Yosemite. He'd be damned if he'd let Corinne sit in a smelly car.

The teens swarmed the car. James bought a soda from them, then called Jack. "What's our normal order on the food? I've got an empty fridge. Didn't check the freezer."

"Like, I'll text you the normal order, man, but you have to put it into the cell phone," said Jack.

James laughed. "I have some time. Getting the car cleaned up after one hell of a smelly job. Fishing followed by hiking. Do you know how to get in?"

"Know where the key is, man. Your brother showed me." The key, along with a vehicle key, was hidden on every vehicle they had, and Mitch's truck was still at the house. James focused; Jack had more to say. "Hey, my cuz, he said he saw Mitch up in Reifert. He was shooting pool at some bar."

"When was this?"

"Two nights ago."

James sighed. Mitch could be anywhere, including crossing several state lines, in two days. Reifert was two hours away. "Thanks for the info. Let me know if anyone sees him again. He's blowing off steam."

"Heard he was, like, hiking? Got caught out in the storm, like a dumbass? And tried to save a corgi mom, but wasn't fast enough, and something about puppies?"

James said, "Wow, the grapevine got the story right for once. He did manage to rescue the puppies, all five, but couldn't save the mom. We've got two puppies and Rachael has three. But, it brought up some old stuff."

"Harsh, dude. So, Mitch kinda went off the rails, cause he misses your guy's mom? And dad? And stuff?"

"And stuff. And the rest of it, too. If you or anyone sees him, call or text me."

"Sure, dude. I'll get the text to you."

"Thanks, Jack."

The SUV gleamed. They'd even vacuumed it out and used cleaner on the inside surfaces. James paid a huge tip, grinned at the high school students who were apparently only a few dollars short of their trip with a line of cars and trucks to wash, and drove to the farm.

Rachael met him as he pulled up. "Thought you would be here like a bat out of hell. But, that shiny SUV was a good idea." She looked down at his leg, the bandage showing on his thigh under his khaki cargo shorts. His tan was so deep that the shorts seemed to merge with his skin. "You can stay, you know. The dogs are having fun getting reacquainted. We can take care of getting Corinne to her appointments, and the satellite guy is supposed to be here today."

James snorted. "Good luck. Never on time." Rachael laughed, and they hugged. They walked towards the outbuilding, his arm around her diminutive shoulders. "I was going to ask you to make yourself useful," she said, as they walked on the opposite side from the goat pen. The kids were climbing the wooden "hills" Gunny and Stretcher had built for them, jumping and making happy goat noises. "We have a tiny house on the far end, there, just past where your lady love is." She pointed, and, sure enough, there was a concrete pour. "The guys are coming in an hour and Gunny and Stretcher will be there, too. But, with that leg...what happened, anyway?" He told her, and she alternated shock and rage at the crazy woman who had attacked James.

Corinne was in a tack room with two fans, a recliner and table liberated from the house, and both dogs, Sheila in the baby sling, and Lucy on her lap. There were piddle pads and bowls of food and water near the door. James found Corinne speaking rapidly in gibberish into her earphones. She stopped talking, stood up, and laughed when he caught up with her in three strides. He hugged her, careful of her shoulder and ribs. She looked down, and said, "What did you do, fillet yourself?" He told her the story, and Corinne's eyes narrowed. "Give me two minutes. She'd be begging me to stop."

"Down, angel." James kissed her. "Got a text on my way here. The cops caught up with her at her house and arrested her."

"Good. Love you, but go away. The site is coming together, and my JavaScript is actually working!"

"Far be it from me to interfere with working JavaScript. I've got a tiny house to help build, then I'll take a look at a good location for a boathouse." He kissed Corinne again. She sat back down, and he followed Rachael out of the tackroom.

"Boathouse?" asked Rachael.

"Christmas present." Rachael caught him in a hug, and he grinned. "Show me where you want the damn boathouse, woman." Rachael grinned, and dragged him off towards the lake.

～

*T*he tiny house plans were lovely. There was a banquette with a foldout table, storage underneath. The banquette could double as a bed with the table folded up, and the right side moved in. The galley kitchen had boat-style storage everywhere it could be. There were two electric burners, powered by solar panels on the roof. There was a composting toilet and a tiny shower. There were double ladders leading to double lofts with beds, and a lot of under-floor storage. James alternated being pissed about working on his lieu days and taking comfort in learning new skills. They made the shell first, Gunny with his booming laugh, the two builders from the tiny house company, James, and Stretcher. They got the walls up and the roof on.

They had installed the kitchen cabinets and the banquette when James had to go out for another long hike, four days. The hikers were birdwatchers with a lot of starts and stops, and camping all three nights. James sent texts to his brother, but only received a single, terse *Shut up, bro, still alive* text for his trouble. He gave up trying.

Nights with Corinne were strange, in his old room with the extra-long bed. Happily, Rachael hadn't frozen it in time, giving them all their old awards, baseballs, and other boy detritus when they moved out. The rock bands and baseball greats posters were long gone. The walls were cornflower blue, the sheets and pillowcases a darker blue. They cuddled, but sex was impossible without injuring both of them. Corinne was exhausted but exhilarated. "I have no idea why I'm getting so much more work done. It's like I'm in a groove. In flow." She made a movement with her hand, like skimming over clear water.

"You have no responsibilities. Household ones. Still have them for your company, of course."

"That is excellent. But, I do feed and water the pups." She grinned. Said pups were sleeping with their brothers, engaging in tussles from time to time, in the great room. "I've tried cleaning up after them, but Rachael gave me a talking-to about bending down with a messed-up shoulder and cracked ribs. I told her the doc has me walking without the sling, and doing what he calls 'gorilla swings'." She made a gorilla sound, and laughed.

"That's the Rachael we know and love. I'm sorry about..."

Corinne put a hand over his mouth. "Don't you go apologizing for Mitch. He knows perfectly well he's being an asshole." James nodded, then licked her hand, making her squeak. "Eww!" She said, wiping her hand on her shorts.

James kissed her. "I heard he's hanging out in biker bars and shooting pool."

Corinne sighed. "I really love him. But, he's using his edges to cut, and he left me when I needed him. I hate to say it, but..."

It was James' turn to put two fingers over Corinne's mouth. "Please, don't make a decision quite yet. He's going through over a decade of emotions he's stuffed. He stopped growing up at twelve. It made me older, and it kind of made him...younger." He took his fingers away, but she snatched them back and kissed them.

Corinne sighed. "I'll withhold judgment for now, but he's being an asshole, and knows it."

"Agreed. He's damaged his relationship with me, too. He'll have to work damn hard to build back the bridges he's burned." He caressed Corinne's face. "I love you. Please, please don't leave us both. I'll move out, buy my own place." He grinned. "We can stay in a very tiny house on Rachael's property. After all, I helped build it." He smiled at her. "The puppies will like being with their brothers, and we can help out around here if needed."

"You have thought about this. Your heart must be breaking. Don't worry about it." She kissed him lightly, then deeply. "I like you." She kissed him again. "I love you." She kissed him again. "I claim you." She smiled, then kissed him deeply.

"Can I claim you back?" asked James, when they came up for air.

"Of course," said Corinne. And, he did.

~

*T*he next day, James went out on another trip. Corinne spent the morning making her JavaScript do cartwheels, then ate lunch outside. Gunny, Rachael, Stretcher, and Corinne passed around fried chicken, biscuits with honey and butter, and salad with pink lemonade to drink. They fell on their food like wolves while the dogs played in the sun, chasing each other, tails wagging. "Seems like we've had them forever," Rachael said about the dogs.

"Seems the same to me," said Corinne. A cloud passed over the sun. "I'm worried about Mitch."

"He can take care of himself," said Stretcher.

"He's being an idiot," said Gunny.

"Welcome to my world," said Rachael. "I love him like breathing.

Was there when he was born, his first change. I was there when Dawn died, and took two sad little boys home. I tried the counseling route, but neither one of them would go. They both kept walking out, refusing to speak, all of it. They were too angry. Mitch found every reason for being angry all the way until we tried to pay for college, and both of them refused it. Mitch blamed Gunny for neither one of them being able to join the military to pay for school themselves, for fear that one or the other brother would die, leaving the other alone."

"That's horrible," said Corinne. Gunny flinched.

"I've never said I wasn't wrong. Stupid, short-sighted. The Marines were great for me and made me into what I am now." Gunny sighed, looked out into the yard, seeing none of it. "I apologized from Day One, but neither one of them heard it."

Corinne shook her head. "Let me repeat myself for the last time. Clusterfuck." Gunny barked out a surprised laugh. "No decision made by anyone could have had a good outcome. There was also no way to figure out which one was less horrible than another one. My friends Tania and Kandace went through their own ones. I...well, it sound stupid and such a first-world problem, but my parents saw me as a doll, or maybe a chess piece. Tania told me to have them pay my way through a master's degree, give me a great start, that it was the least they could do for me."

Corinne grinned lopsidedly. "I got to pay it forward, with both of them, here and there, where I could. They're both saddled with debt, but with much less than they could have had, and that's how I got to keep them with me through graduate school. Small clusterfuck, but we did the best we could." She leaned over, and stared into Gunny's eyes. "So, stop beating yourself up. You did the best you could with impossible choices. James let it go. Mitch needs to let it go. If you quit using your guilt to beat yourself up, it may make it easier for Mitch to let go." Corinne sipped from her glass of pink lemonade.

Rachael wiped away tears, then looked at Gunny. She put her hand on Gunny's hand. "Love, she's right. Let's both let it go."

Gunny nodded once, his eyes bright. "We were lucky when you came to town," he said to Corinne.

Corinne blushed over her glass, then she put it down. Rachael grabbed her hand. "We are very lucky."

Corinne shook her head. "Both Mitch and James rescued me."

"No," said Rachael. "You rescued us."

Stretcher blew out a raspberry, and said, "Wah wah wah." She stood and stalked back into the kitchen. Everyone laughed.

# AFTERMATH

The next day, Stretcher took Corinne to throwing practice in the woods, then physical therapy. Stretcher left her at the A-frame house after James texted Corinne. *Coming home. Stay at the house. I'll pick you up, pick up what you wanted to take back.*

Corinne texted back. *You better get us back before dinner. Chinese takeout tonight.* He sent her a hungry face emoji, then a chopsticks one.

Corinne entered, locked the door behind her, then realized someone was already there. Malcolm grinned, green eyes slitted with rage. "Miss me?" He leaned against the couch. He had a thing in his hand that he snapped, and it turned into a baton.

"A man who threw my pack over the side of a mountain, smashed my cell phone, all deliberately, and then tried to beat the crap out of me?" Corinne slipped her hands into her pockets and leaned against the door on her good shoulder and side. She snorted. "Hardly. What was supposed to be next? Beating the crap out of me? Murder?"

Malcolm stalked forward. "You need to pay."

Corinne shook her head, her eyes on Malcolm. His weapon would extend his reach. "For what? All my money goes to pay off debt. I don't keep much on me. I have twenty and about three quarters." She pulled the money out of her right pocket, trying not to grimace. She'd left her sling in Stretcher's car, as the doctor had pronounced it time to keep it off. She dropped the money on the floor.

Malcolm sneered. "You filed charges against me, bitch," he said, stalking forward. "Had to find you first, but now I've got you. My word against yours."

Corinne shook her head again. "Nope, got your fingerprints on my phone before you smashed it." She grinned. "Buh-bye." She stood tall, pulled the throwing knife out of its hidden pocket, and then she threw. The knife poked out of his eye. Malcolm staggered, fell. The baton slipped from his fingers with a clatter. Corinne reached back, unlocked the door, exited it, went out to the carport, stumbled to a bush, and threw up. She wiped her mouth, then her eyes with her other hand, grimacing through the pain. She leaned against the wall on her good shoulder, texted Stretcher, and dialed 9-1-1.

～

Stretcher arrived first on her bike. She looked in the window, grunted, and stood next to Corinne. The cops arrived, and the woman, Officer Perez, who was short but fierce, interviewed Corinne. The second officer, Officer Balanca, a tall man with wide shoulders, looked in the window, then called the sheriff, who called the state police. Stretcher described Corinne's injuries, and insisted that she be allowed to sit. After a call to her doctor, they let Corinne sit on a chair brought out from Mitch's Harley garage, which had been against the little desk Mitch used for taking orders and billing. The officers questioned the women, then switched places to question them again. Then the homicide detectives started in with their questions.

A woman in a black SUV drove up, Gunny's SUV right behind her. Gunny got out of his car, and walked to kneel beside Corinne's chair. A woman got out of the black SUV, dressed in a black suit with a tapered skirt and flat shoes. Her black hair was in a high ponytail, and she looked pissed. She walked right up to Corinne and said, "I'm Olivia Rambran. Give me a dollar." Stretcher gave Corinne a dollar, and Olivia took the dollar from Corinne. "My client has answered the same questions..."

"Five times," said Corinne.

"Five times. She's in a great deal of pain from seeing a doctor, X-rays, and physical therapy from her first attack by the same man. Charges were filed. If you have any more questions, and not the same ones she's answered five times, you may speak to me, and I will set up an appointment with my client." She handed out her card. "Now, my client is leaving."

Stretcher helped Corinne to her feet. "Come on. We've got a nice bed for you to sleep in."

A Harley came flying around the last curve, past the coroner's van, and all the cop cars. Mitch parked, and took off his helmet. He got off, and ran towards them. "Corinne! Are you alright? Where's your sling?"

Stretcher got in front of Corinne. Corinne tapped her shoulder, and Stretcher yawned, then moved away. "I love you," said Corinne. "But, I was just attacked again. Stretcher taught me how to throw a knife, and so I was able to defend myself. I just...killed his ass. Threw a knife in his eye." She shuddered, then stood up tall again.

"What?" Mitch looked over at Stretcher, who nodded.

"I learned how to do it to prove to myself I could, and because it isn't just James that left. You had to go into town for parts at the picky part place at the motorcycle graveyard, stuff like that, then you left mentally, and then physically." Mitch held himself against her onslaught of words. "Then, I realized I couldn't count on you. When you were here, you were somewhere else in your head, someplace angry and dark. Get some damn medicine if you need it, talk to a therapist, contemplate your navel. But, you haven't been here for a long time. Certainly not just now when I was attacked again. You. Weren't. There," Corinne said, poking his chest. She walked around him. Stretcher helped her into Gunny's vehicle.

Stretcher closed the door, and Gunny stepped up, and towered over Mitch. "You can hate me three times a day, and four on week-ends. Great, fine. But, you left this amazing woman when she needed you most. Pop your head out of your ass, boy." He turned to

Olivia Rambran. "Counselor, I thank you. Send the bill to the house." He got into the truck and pulled out, leaving Mitch in the dust.

~

*M*itch followed them to the farm. He couldn't stay at the house, with the cops still crawling all over, taking pictures. He was shaken, but he focused as he drove. He followed, parked the bike, and was too late to open the door for Corinne. He couldn't open the door to the house because he no longer had a key. He remembered where they hid it, but Gunny got to the door and opened it with a single movement. Gunny held open the door while Rachael and Stretcher got Corinne into the house. "May I enter?" Mitch asked Gunny.

"You hurt her, you're sleeping in the barn, or better still a hotel, boy." Mitch nodded. Once inside, Mitch got a glass of lemonade for Corinne, and Stretcher got her pills. Corinne took four—three was her maximum dose—and Stretcher popped the recliner up for her.

Corinne looked at Mitch. "I'm too damn tired, shaky, and in pain to deal with you, I suggest helping out with the tiny house in back. Bring my computer here first."

"I'll tell you where it is," said Rachael.

"I've got to do a pour for the boathouse," said Gunny. "You need anything, Corinne, my phone is on me." He kissed her cheek, and strode out the back door.

Rachael pointed out the back window to the barn. She looked into his eyes. "You piss her off, you piss me off," she said. "And, I'm done apologizing. We did our best with you, and you moved away at seventeen. I loved your mama and Nick at least as much as you did, but in a different way. We lost them, then we lost you. I think you need to take a hard look at yourself. I think your parents would hate where you are now in your head. The computer is in the tack room." She opened the back door for him.

Mitch picked his jaw up off the floor, and strode out. The door clicked shut behind him. He took out his phone. *Bro, Corinne nearly got killed by Malcolm the Demon. He's dead. Caught a case of a knife in the eye.*

*WTF? Corinne all right?* texted James.

*Not hurt. Gunny called Livie Rambran and got her sprung from police questioning. Our girl is sore, on Rachael's couch. She took some meds and now she's gonna sleep. I am getting her computer for her.*

*Bet she gave you what for,* James guessed.

*Did. Everybody else did too—Rachael, Gunny, and the damned cat.* Mitch had to stop texting when he was attacked by five tumbling puppies. "Everyone's a critic," he said, kneeling, to dig his way out of the mass of doggy joy. He petted and rolled with them, enjoying their happy barks. "Missed you too."

Mitch checked his phone. James was terse, and obviously pissed off. *Called Livie and got the lowdown. Can't get away for another two hours. Stick nearby. Will pick up Chinese for everybody.* Mitch vaguely remembered that Livie the lawyer was a year ahead of him, and therefore a classmate of his brother James. James had considered becoming a cop, but didn't when a local cop was killed during a simple traffic stop on a rainy night during their senior year in high school. His brother would never leave him, so he couldn't join the cops or the military. Guilt ate at Mitch once again.

Mitch stopped his trip down memory lane. He entered the tack house, and was insanely careful with Corinne's rig. He got the computer separated from the two screens on little tables on either side of the recliner. He was careful with the wires and the power cord. He got it all together, and avoided tripping over five puppies on his way back across the yard. He entered by the back door, closed it, and quietly made his way over to the little TV tray and set up Corinne's computer. He plugged it in, very quietly, because Corinne was either asleep or pretending to be out cold.

He went out the back, and strode over towards the tiny house. There was a man and woman on the roof wearing hard hats installing solar panels. He stood below them, and said, "Ahoy the house!"

The people didn't stop doing what they were doing. "This is tricky," said the woman.

"I'm Mitch. Gunny sent me to help in any way I could."

"About done," said the man. "Sorry."

"Thanks." Mitch sighed, and headed towards the greenhouse. Inside, it was a riot of green and crimson, gold, and more. They practiced vertical farming, and there were fat white plastic pipes filled with water, plants sticking out of holes. LED lights in red, green, blue, and white ran across metal tubes over each grid, and heat lamps were in a cabinet in the back for winter. Some were vertical, some horizontal, all laid out in grids. It looked like a pipe factory had sprouted herbs and vegetables. Rachael was picking fat tomatoes, her eyes narrowed as she cut them off the plant with a quick snip of her cutter. "I'm not useful to the tiny house people," said Mitch. "What do you want me to do?"

Rachael stood, and looked him right in the eyes. "Apologize."

Mitch blinked. "I left at seventeen, and didn't think about how that would hurt you."

Rachael huffed out a laugh. "I forgave you years ago. You were a twisted mess, and you had to be the one to untwist yourself, since you wouldn't receive either my love or my help. No, I meant Corinne. I have no idea if you can salvage your relationship with her, but that's a good start."

"She's asleep," said Mitch. He nodded at Rachael. "I'll just... Where is the boathouse?"

"Oh, my." Rachael stood, took her basket of tomatoes, and exited the greenhouse. She pointed. "By the dock."

Mitch hauled himself to the side of the lake, Gunny was pounding in stakes to mark out the boathouse. The land had already been leveled. "Don't bother, boy," said Gunny. "I did you wrong. But..."

Mitch held up a hand. "I knew Corinne was right when she said it."

"Clusterfuck," said Gunny.

"A good word for it. I had to shed the anger. I followed an MMA fighter around for a while and learned from him. Worked out in gyms in four counties." He rubbed the back of his neck. "It took losing a bout to get it through my skull that the anger was never going to leave. It's at them for dying, at you for your role in it."

Mitch held up a hand when Gunny opened his mouth. "Dad signed the papers, not you, and he didn't just do whatever you said. He must have thought he was doing the right thing at the time." He sighed. "Anger at me, for being a dick for years. At Rachael, for being so loving, despite how I treated her. At me some more, for never getting any damn help." He barked out a laugh. "At Corinne, for loving the hell out of me, and getting it through my skull for once that I was wrong, dead wrong."

Gunny stood up, did nothing to stop the flow of words. Mitch sighed gustily. "I tried to let it go, but it didn't go. I just gave up and went home, hoping I would find some way to...live with it? Ignore it?" Then I saw the cop cars, and I..." His eyes filled with tears. "I could have lost her, Gunny, if she hadn't been so pigheaded to learn to defend herself while she was in massive pain. I left her alone, trying not to strike out at her with my stupid anger." Gunny stepped forward, and grabbed Mitch in a bear hug. Mitch let the tears fall, and Gunny just held on.

~

Corinne woke up to the smell of rice, noodles, oranges, and black pepper. "Chinese food!" she said, and started to sit up. She gasped and lay back.

"Lay still, dumbass," said James, his voice rough. He spread the bags of food across several TV trays, and knelt down beside Corinne. He helped her move the feet of the recliner down to help her sit up, took her face in his hands, and kissed her. "I love you. You will not be nearly killed by an armed asshole when I'm gone, ever again." He kissed her again, once, twice.

"He never touched me," Corinne mimicked her throw. "Right through the eye. Poom."

James scrunched up his face. "Eww. Gross."

Corinne pushed his shoulder with her good hand. "Dumbass." He grinned and kissed her again.

"Done yet?" asked Mitch. "I've got to wash and cut up the salad.

Cucumber and bell pepper." He held up a small basket. He grinned. "Be right back with the slice and dice, or slice and hack, in my case." He turned, and headed towards the kitchen.

Corinne laughed. "I want to kill him, yet I laugh. What the hell is wrong with me?"

James sighed gustily, and stood up. "I want him dead too, but somehow I can't actually kill him." He stepped forward, and started taking little paper boxes out of the bags.

"I call dibs on the orange chicken," said Corinne.

"You can't call dibs, and I bought a triple order. Plus broccoli pepper beef, moo shu pork, and General Tso's Chicken. Triple on everything."

"Smart," said Stretcher, padding in on bare feet. She sat on the other end of the recliner. "Pass me some chopsticks."

James sat in between Stretcher and Corinne. Mitch came in with the salad, plates, and spoons. "Hey, now I gotta pull over a chair." He put the food down on another foldout table, pulled over a fat chair, and sat down on Corinne's bad side. He put some of the cucumber pepper salad on each plate, and passed them to James. James filled them up with rice, noodles, and the various Chinese dishes, except for the mu shu pork. Stretcher used an empty plate to lay out the Chinese pancakes, put the mu shu pork in the middle, and added hoisin sauce. She rolled each up like a burrito with quick, expert movements. Stretcher passed them out to the various plates.

Gunny opened the back door for Rachael. All five dogs tumbled in and attacked their toys in front of the fireplace. Rachael passed out doggie snacks so they didn't beg during dinner, washed up, and joined them at the TV trays. Gunny washed up as well. They sang, dug in, and said absolutely nothing as they consumed the food. Afterward, Mitch cleaned up while everyone else groaned and lay in various states of relaxation on the tufted chairs and the couch. The dogs followed Mitch, hoping for Chinese food, but they got puppy chow instead, wet food mixed with dry.

They moved the chairs around to face the television, and they had a rock-paper-scissors over the movie about the Olympic climber who fell in love with a woman who was secretly a spy, the series about a school for gifted alien children with their first human students, and the cop buddy show about the fairy queen and her enforcers who kept the law of the Fairy Court. Everyone got a dog to pet, even Stretcher, and they watched the cop buddy show first. Corinne fell asleep halfway through the third episode. They finished the episode, and by mutual unspoken agreement, Rachael, Gunny, and Stretcher silently crept out of the room.

James covered Corinne with a sheet, put the sleeping Lucy back on her lap, and went to the back door. Mitch sighed, and followed. "No," said James, in a whisper. "You're with her until you make it up to her. Or she chooses not to be with you anymore." He punched his brother's arm. "Don't screw this up. I don't want to have to move us out." He sighed. "Hell, I want to move out, and it's my house too. Kind of hate your face right now.

Mitch nodded once, hard. "I get that. I won't screw this up."

"Spirit help us." James rolled his eyes.

"I'm sorry I was an ass. For over a decade."

James punched his brother in the arm, then held him close. "Then stop," he said, into his brother's ear. "Just. Stop."

"I will," whispered Mitch.

"I've got to go before I punch you a lot of times." James went out the back door.

Mitch went to the linen closet in the hallway, and got out a sheet. Sheila and Rascal followed him. "You can sleep with me," he said to them. He threw the sheet over his shoulder, picked up a puppy in each hand, and accepted their kisses. He walked back to the couch, sat down, pushed back the recliner on the other end, put the dogs down next to him, then sat back up. He went to the kitchen and brought out a glass of lemonade. He put it next to Corinne's pills. He was unsurprised to see Sheila snuggling at Corinne's hip, and equally unsurprised to see three more doggy faces peering up at him when he sat down. He lifted them up, and they arranged themselves on his lap, leg, and hip. Mitch read a book on his cell phone for a while, a spy thriller about a woman who could transform herself into nearly anyone via makeup and wigs. He slipped into sleep.

~

*M*itch awoke to Corinne's gasp. She carefully sat up, and moved a sleeping Lucy to a spot next to Sheila. Mitch followed her gaze, and saw through the window the gray wolf with a white muzzle and ink-black nose slip forward, slinking its way closer and closer to the light. Its eyes were crystal blue. Mitch opened the door while Corinne sat up completely, then stood. She looked down, found her pills and lemonade, and swallowed three pills with a single gulp. She stepped forward, and walked through the door out into the yard. Mitch followed, and closed the door behind him.

The wolf sniffed Corinne's hand. She laughed. He chuffed out his own laugh. He danced a little to the left, and to the right. Corinne smiled, and danced with him.

The wolf stared right at Mitch, and chuffed. It took seconds for Mitch to peel off his shirt, jeans, underwear, and socks, then change. He changed into a smaller version of his brother. Both wolves sat down next to Corinne. Corinne knelt, then looked into the larger gray wolf's deep blue eyes. "We've claimed each other," she said. "Forever claimed." The wolf licked her hand.

Corinne looked into the gray wolf with considerably more black on the tips of his soft coat, a tiny bit smaller than his brother. "If you let your anger let us down again, then we're through," she said to the darker wolf. "We're nearly through now. You're hanging by a single thread. You'll have to make it up to me, be actually with us in your head, not just physically. Attend anger management classes, and go to counseling, get some meds if you need them. One screwup, and that tiny house over there's mine." Mitch put his head on his paws, bowing to her. She patted his head. "I claim you too, and you claim me, if you survive the tightrope of the next few months of you making it up to us." The wolf ran his head down her jawline, licked her. "Forever claimed," Corinne said. The darker wolf sat back and howled, but not in pain, rage, or fear. It was a howl of pure joy.

A muscular mountain lion padded around from the side of the house, stretched lazily, climbed up on the porch, and lay there, twitching its tail. "Stretcher, you're lovely," Corinne said. The cat purred.

A huge silvery wolf came around the side of the house, much bigger than the other two. Both wolves promptly bared their throats to him. A female in silver and white came from around the other side of the house. The smaller wolves bared their throats to her, too. The larger wolves sat, and regally watched as the smaller wolves circled each other, yipping, snapping and biting one another. The largest wolf growled, and they separated, then chased each other around the yard. The wolves danced under the moonlight.

The two larger wolves stepped forward, and the female one started to race. She bounded over the fence, and the others followed her, streaking out under the moonlight. Corinne watched them until they disappeared into the trees.

Corinne turned, and walked to the mountain lion. She stroked her giant head, scratched her behind the ears, and the lion chuffed, then purred. "I'm going to bed. I assume you'll stand guard?" The mountain lion chuffed again. "I wish I could be like you, but, apparently, I don't have the genetics." The mountain lion pushed on Corinne's hand. "I'm going, I'm going." She walked towards the door.

She turned, and walked back to the puma. "I'll keep the secret, protect you all, if I can," said Corinne. "I may be a puny human, but I love you guys. Love them." She sighed, groaned. "Now if I can get this damn shoulder to heal..." She walked in the house, and shut the door. The mountain lion swished her tail, and stood guard.

∽

*M*itch was the one to move out. He stayed at the tiny house at night for two weeks, then went away to some anger management camp. He came back a lot calmer, and on a low dose of antidepressants. He moved into the tiny house again. He saw a counselor twice a week and was in a group of other sad, angry people. Corinne let him move back in at three months, provided he did his proper chores and was present in spirit as well as in body. He still threw the occasional wrench out in the garage, and kickboxed nearly every day. But, he was an attentive lover, and he made strides in most of his relationships.

James wasn't so fast to forgive his brother. "She could have died, man. Malcolm would never have been able to hide in the house with you here."

"Yes, he would have. My brain wasn't here, either." Mitch sighed. "I can't keep beating myself up over it. It's actions, you know?"

"You mean, actually making breakfast for our woman?" They were drinking hot apple cider out on the porch. Mitch was off alcohol because of his medication. The night was frigid. They sat bundled in their winter coats, snow falling in clumps from the trees with wet plops.

"Laundry, sweeping up, cleaning up after the dogs." They heard Lucy whine inside the house, and they both laughed. "I have one guy in the group, lost both parents to cancer, now his wife has it."

"Rough."

"Tell me about it. Another guy lost his kid to a drunk driver. I think of all the times I drove drunk or angry, or both...I just full-body cringe. I was on a bike, too. There are no old, bold bikers, man. I was trying to take myself out, I think. Not actively suicidal, just reckless and really stupid. Then Corinne opened me up like a tin can, and all my pain got out. Made me angry all over again."

"That's our woman." James looked out at the sun setting over the trees. "She opened my tin can too, you know. I used being outdoors as a balm, soothed my soul."

"I forgot to do that. We live in heaven, you know. But I wasn't looking. Stupid."

"Stupid." James smiled as his brother snorted. "Hey, I was agreeing with you!"

"Anyway, it's not a quick thing. I'm not cured, bro. Gonna need to take my own loner rides, camp and hike. I'm setting ones up with the people from my group. Not just guys, you know. Females get wound real tight, too. Some of them are ex-soldiers. I'm gonna make some bikes for them, get them out to see the country they defended."

"Normally, I'd rant and rave at you about leaving us. But, you gotta do what you gotta do, preferably before winter sets in harder. We've got Rachael and Stretcher to help, and our woman is mostly healed."

Mitch looked back over his shoulder. "Our girl's worth it. You're worth it. Our family is worth it. The people in my group are worth it too, except for one. He's an alcoholic, won't get help. One of the females is going to take him to a meeting. Hope it takes."

"I hope so too. Wow. My brother, caring about people other than himself."

Mitch pushed on James' shoulder. "Hey, I was a self-centered asshole. Please make sure I don't go down that path again."

James' eyes turned flat, bleak. "I tried, bro. You gotta do a better job of listening. I can't tell you how many times I wanted to dump you the lake, in your clothes, in winter. No one could tell you a thing. I stayed to keep you from...from killing yourself, man. If I had gone..." He rubbed the tears out of his eyes.

"Bro." Mitch hugged his brother. "Sorry. Was trying to make you responsible for me again." They watched the sunset. "So, how's that boathouse coming? I see you got it up and roofed. Can I help with the insides?" They sat and talked boathouses until Corinne and two puppies dragged them in to watch movies.

# EPILOGUE

The ceremony was held in the same meadow where Corinne and James had their picnic, but now it was moonlight. An enormous female grizzly, a great horned owl, and a great golden python joined them, outside the circle. Everyone else was in human form, except Corinne, as she'd always had only one form. Corinne wore a white dress that fell in long lines to her ankles and white boots, with long sleeves that covered her hands with holes for her thumbs. The gray outlines of her wolf on her right shoulder and the black dog on her left showed under the dress, surrounded by secret symbols hidden in Celtic knots. Rachael wore the same dress, in red. The rest wore jeans, leather jackets, and boots. It was fall, and the crimson and gold of the trees could be seen when the torchlight hit them from the torches in their holders at the north, south, east, and west.

Rachael stepped forward, the circle tightening in response. "Spirit moves me to bring one not of our number into our family. Does anyone have Spirit speaking to them about this?"

James stepped forward. "This woman held off two attacks by herself, so she has proven her strength. She has begun and run her own business, so she has proven she can support herself and others in times of need. She had shown great compassion and humility, coupled with a refusal to take any crap, necessary among us to survive." Everyone chuffed a laugh, except the snake, who hissed.

Gunny stepped forward. "She has shown an amazing propensity to heal damaged minds and hearts. I have seen this with my own eyes." He stepped back.

Stretcher stalked forward. "This woman can learn, take direction, and excel." She stepped back.

Mitch stepped forward. "This woman has healed me, allowed me to work thorough years of rage and stupid behavior." He stepped back.

James stepped forward again. "She is steady as a rock, stronger than granite, with a clear, bright heart. She loves absolutely, and keeps our laws and secrets." He stepped back.

"Spirit moves me to accept this woman as our own, to keep our secrets, even at the price of her own life. To stand by us, help in times of need. To raise our children as Changed, with our laws and strictures." She looked out at the owl, bear, and snake. "Do the Changed Clans object?" The great horned owl did not hoot. The bear sat on its hind legs, a huge golden brown grizzly. The python was seemingly inert. Rachael took in two more breaths, then said, "Therefore, by the Spirit that moves within us all, I accept her."

"I accept her," said the rest.

The bear lumbered off, the owl took flight with great beats of enormous wings that made the torches flicker, and the python slithered past the torchlight into the trees. "Well," said Rachael. "Shall we begin?"

They drew inward. Mitch stood on Corinne's left side, and James on her right. Each lifted a hand, and took Corinne's hands in theirs. The brothers put their hands on each other's shoulders, to close the circle. Rachael bound their hands to Corinne's with red ribbons. She stepped back. "Please watch and observe. You will be called upon to support them in any way they need," she said, her voice carrying on the wind.

"We watch and observe, and will give our support," said Gunny,

Stretcher, Rico, Luce, Yancey, and Jared. They surrounded Corinne, James, and Mitch.

"I pledge to you my heart, hearth, and troth," Rachael said, and all three repeated. "I pledge to join with you in times of sadness, joy, and all in between." They repeated again. "I bind myself to you until the winter of our lives buries us under its snows, to rise again with the spring." They repeated the last words together, Corinne's voice high and choked with emotion, James' sure and steady, Mitch's with a growl underneath.

Rachael fought not to join Corinne in her joyous tears. "Then, with great joy, I recommend you to the Spirit that lies within us all, that your spirits be joined in this life, and that you find each other in the next." Rachael unbound their cords, then braided them together to hang over their door. She led them in the ancient chant. It had taken Corinne two weeks to remember all the words, ones that rang through the ages with vows of secrecy, family, and in finding joy in one another.

Gunny and Stretch gathered the torches. Gunny gave one to Rachael and another to Rico, and took up the rear with the last torch, as they all hiked back to the house. There, they had a huge dinner of roast pork with apples and honey, brown sugar carrots, biscuits with butter and honey, and apple pie for dessert, sweet things for a sweet life together.

After dinner, the dogs herded them from table to the great room for dancing, then danced with them. Mitch got the first dance, whirling Corinne around. They laughed, and Corinne was able to move sinuously. Over a year after the first attack, her pain was long gone. She'd been lifting weights and kickboxing, and she was ready to dance. "We're not exactly married," Mitch said, with a grin.

Corinne laughed. "You know perfectly well that, according to the law, I can only marry one of you. And, we've got all the other paper-work for the rest of that stuff." Corinne's old friend Mike, a tax lawyer now expecting a child and working in St. Louis, had created a trust for them, gotten them health and life insurance under Corinne's business, and gotten all their monetary affairs in order. Corinne had finished paying off her debts by using the website she'd created for Rachael and Gunny as a springboard for farms, artists, and small businesses all over the state. She'd finished the last payment the month before.

Mitch sighed, and looked at her longingly. "It was the dog shape. James' wolf is cooler."

Corinne laughed again. "That was exactly it."

Aerosmith's "Angel" stopped, and James tapped Mitch out. James grinned, took Corinne in his arms, and danced to "Thinking Out Loud." Corinne smiled up at James, who leaned down to whisper in her ear. "He is still bugging you about the legal marriage?"

Corinne nodded. "I think he felt kind of hurt, and thought it had something to do with his assholery from earlier."

James barked out a laugh. "Assholery. Love it."

"Still haven't convinced him that he makes more and can afford his own damn insurance, but he just makes this face." Corinne made the same face a now-grown Lucy made when she wanted treats. James laughed again. "Anyhow, the reservation still good?"

"Cabin, check. Really big hot tub, check. Shifter staff, check. Space for us to run while you get yourself done up in the spa, check."

"Lovely," said Corinne. "Dawn," she said.

"Dawn," said James.

They rocked out until dawn. They told stories and drank honey mead, all except for Corinne, who stuck to honey water. Alcohol wouldn't be good for the babies, a boy and girl growing in her belly. One name would be Dawn, the other, Nick, after their deceased parents. Corinne sat and watched Gunny dance, holding Rachael close, watched Stretcher pretend not to care in the corner, watched Rico and Yancey play with the dogs on the floor. It was home and family, forever claimed.

<<<The End>>>

# AFTERWORD

**Thank you!**

Thank you for being one of my beautiful, amazing readers! I can't do what I do without you! If you liked the book, please leave a review! I read them all, looking to improve my craft so I can write more fun stories for you.

Thank you to my beta reader team, Jodee, Swati, and Manasa. My editors Lynda and iWordyNerdy are amazing, and so is my critique partner, Alyssa. Crooked Sixpence created my incredible covers. Any errors left in the manuscript are entirely my own. Please let me know what they are so I can fix them in your online review! Or, you can contact me on social media at Facebook: Facebook.com/lj.hawke, Instagram: Instagram.com/ljhawke, and Twitter: Twitter.com/Hawkelj, and my website: ljhawkeauthor.com.

**Books in the Forever Loved series:**
Forever Charmed
Forever Claimed
Forever Wild
Forever Challenged

# ABOUT THE AUTHOR

**L. J. Hawke** is an author, university professor, and an avid reader. She writes what she loves to read—paranormal romance, urban fantasy, and science fiction, as well as some nonfiction titles in her fields of expertise. She can be found petting her cats while writing, or with a backpack on her back, traveling the world—after calling the cat sitter.

**One last thing...**

If you enjoyed this book or found it useful, I'd be very grateful if you'd post a short review on Amazon. Your support really does make a difference, and I read all the reviews personally so I can get your feedback and make this book even better.

Thanks again for your support!

facebook.com/lj.hawke
twitter.com/Hawkelj
instagram.com/ljhawke

www.ingramcontent.com/pod-product-compliance
Lightning Source LLC
Chambersburg PA
CBHW071909220626
47052CB00002B/275